A Gangsta's Paradise

Lock Down Publications and Ca$h
Presents

A Gangsta's Paradise
A Novel by *Trai'Quan*

A Gangsta's Paradise

Lock Down Publications
Po Box 944
Stockbridge, Ga 30281

Visit our website @
www.lockdownpublications.com

Copyright 2022 by Trai'Quan
A Gangsta's Paradise

Lock Down Publications
Like our page on Facebook: Lock Down Publications @
www.facebook.com/lockdownpublications.ldp
Book interior design by: **Shawn Walker**
Edited by: **Jill Alicea**

Stay Connected with Us!

Text **LOCKDOWN** to 22828 to stay up-to-date with new releases, sneak peaks, contests and more...
Thank you.

Submission Guideline.

Submit the first three chapters of your completed manuscript to ldpsubmissions@gmail.com, subject line: Your book's title. The manuscript must be in a .doc file and sent as an attachment. Document should be in Times New Roman, double spaced and in size 12 font. Also, provide your synopsis and full contact information. If sending multiple submissions, they must each be in a separate email.

Have a story but no way to send it electronically? You can still submit to LDP/Ca$h Presents. Send in the first three chapters, written or typed, of your completed manuscript to:

LDP: Submissions Dept
Po Box 944
Stockbridge, Ga 30281

DO NOT send original manuscript. Must be a duplicate.

Provide your synopsis and a cover letter containing your full contact information.

Thanks for considering LDP and Ca$h Presents.

Trai'Quan

Prologue

Two little boys were riding their bikes through the projects. They rode until they came to an empty building that looked old and decrepit. The building was boarded up and had been that way for quite some time. The place looked scary to the young boys as they stopped and stared at the building.

"What you want to do? You want to go in there and see what it look like on the inside?" asked one boy to the other.

"Shit, nigga, I ain't muthafucking scared," the other boy said.

"Nigga, I ain't scared of nothing," the first boy replied as he jumped off his bike and threw it to the ground.

"Fuck this shit, let's do this." Dropping his bike also, as they walked towards the empty building.

Their names were James Boldmen and Jarvis Green. They had been friends since they could remember and they loved to challenge each other. Neither of them expected this to be a challenge that would change their lives forever.

Once they reached the building, they noticed that one of the windows had a board that was down near hanging off, so they easily removed it and headed inside the building. Once they were inside, they walked around from room to room.

The place was filthy and smelled like shit. A few rats ran around the floor.

"Damn, this muthafuckin' building stanks," said James, putting his hand over his nose.

"It smells like shit in here," Jarvis said in response.

They heard a noise in another part of the building and both of them froze and looked at each other. Both were shocked and couldn't move.

"You heard that?" Jarvis asked.

"Yeah, man." James moved towards the direction noise came from.

They walked through a doorway until they came to an open area. A mattress was on the floor and the room was filled with trash. A woman and a man were buck-ass naked, fucking hard and strong on top of the mattress. They both were moaning and didn't notice the two young boys watching them having sex. Both the boys smiled to each other while they watched the two people fucking.

"Gotdamn junkies, what the fuck y'all doing in this building?" Jarvis yelled at the two people having sex.

They were so shocked that they both looked up at once. The man looked from one boy to another.

"What the fuck y'all little punks doing in this building?" he said as he grabbed his pants and started to put them on.

The boys were staring at the naked woman, who continued to lay there with her legs open. She looked into James's eyes and would not let go. He began to feel his penis harden underneath his clothes. Jarvis watched the woman's wet spot between her legs.

"What the fuck y'all little punks looking at? Oh, I got something for y'all muthafuckas!" The man went over to a corner and reached under a bunch of trash on the floor and came up with a gun.

Both the boys broke into a run from the room and made it away back to the window that they had used to come into the building. James made it out, but Jarvis was grabbed from behind by the man with the gun in his hand.

"You young punk bitch!" yelled the man as he threw him to the ground.

Jarvis yelled for his friend to help him. "James!"

Hearing his friend yelling his name made him stop and turn to look back at the building he had just made it out of. Then he turned to look around to see if anyone was outside who could maybe help, but no one was in sight. He then ran back into the building, but not before spotting a brick the size of a football and grabbing it before climbing back into the window.

Once he was inside, he saw the man standing over his friend, yelling, "What's up now, huh? You little punk bitch!"

James wasted no time. He hit the man over the head with the brick as hard as he could. Blood went everywhere, but this didn't stop James. He kept beating the man in the head until he was completely unconscious. The gun had flown from the man's hand when he went down. The woman could hear the beating from the other room. Jarvis jumped up from the ground and went to stumping the man in the head. James went over to where the gun had fell and picked it up, tucking it in his waist, heading into the room where the woman was. Jarvis stomped the sleeping man a few more times, yelling, "You the punk bitch!" just before he spit on the man. Then he followed his friend into the other room.

The woman sat on the mattress, still not attempting to cover herself up. Her eyes were big and she was staring at the two boys as they walked in. James looked her over until he felt his penis start to get hard again. He then cracked a smile, looking into the woman's eyes. The woman smiled back and then licked her lips. She then threw her legs open and said, "If y'all muthafuckers want some pussy, then come and get it."

Both the boys looked at each other, then made a move towards the woman. That was the day both of them would lose their virginity.

James Boldman grew up in the projects. He had no brothers or sisters. He was the only child. His mother never told him who his father was and he never met any aunts or uncles. His mother was the type of woman to leave for weeks and never tell him where she was going. The rumors around his hood were that she could be bought with the right amount of money. The word was that she wasn't cheap, and she was no junkie type of bitch. She wore the best clothes and always had hella jewelry on. The only fucked up part was that she never bought her only son much of anything.

He had to make his own way in life, she told him. "Nothing in life is free," she would always say to him while counting money. She made sure food was on the table, but he would get no gifts other than holidays.

From the moment that he learned how to get money, he hustled, and he never stopped remembering what his mother would say to him. He had a way with the girls, so she gave him the nickname "Pretty-Boy." He let this name stick, only because his mother gave it to him. Even with his mother being secretive and despite her selfish ways, he still loved her dearly. It broke his heart a million times over when one day his mother left on one of her outings and never came back, leaving him alone in this cold and tragic world.

And at the tender age of fourteen, PrettyBoy was forced to be a man, and although it was exceedingly hard, he vowed to be not just a man, but THE MAN!

Chapter 1
The Mac-11 Crew

It all started Saturday night at 11:30 p.m. The city was Atlanta - Hotlanta to those who really knew the city. The night life was wild, and hell, even the freaks said it all. Days and nights where people in the city did whatever the fuck they wanted. They always did say that "the freaks come out at night".

That's exactly what PrettyBoy James was thinking as he drove his candy apple red '91 Chevy Caprice through the club's parking lot. The club was S.O.'s, famous for the college crowd – well, at least the college girls. Then again, it wouldn't have been much of a club if the ballers from the hood didn't come. Not to worry though, because they were definitely in the building tonight.

S.O.'s was a club that sat right on the street corner in downtown Atlanta, a brick building with S.O.'s written in bright lights right on the front of the building. Under the club's name were two huge glass doors, and a red rope made a line to the side of the building. There was another one right in front of the club's door, and that was for VIPs only. In front of all this stood two men in black. They were the club's bouncers, and they both were two big black ugly muthafuckas. The club was replete tonight. There was a line of people from the front of the club almost all the way to the back. To PrettyBoy James, it looked like most of the people that were in line were women – or "hoes", if you went by what he and his boys called them.

"Gotdamn, my nigga, you see all them hoes?" That was Mike, PrettyBoy's main partner, who was sitting in the passenger seat.

"Hell yeah," answered Jarvis and Mac from the backseat.

Jarvis and Mac were cousins, but they didn't look anything alike. Jarvis was dark-skinned, six feet tall, and was nothing but skin and bones. Mac was light-skinned, 5'7", and cut up from working out. Nevertheless, they had one thing in common . They both considered themselves to be some real playas. The whole team knew that they were all down for each other. They had proved it through all the run-ins with the law and fights they'd had with other crews. The crew had been through hell and back. Hell, if they weren't partners, then who were?

11

PrettyBoy finally found a parking space and pulled in. By the time he took the gun off his lap and began putting it under his seat, Mike had already done the same with his Colt 45. They both carried the same type of gun. They had bought them together from some white dude that came to the hood with a truck full of guns. Jarvis and Mac didn't bring guns to the club tonight. Mac didn't feel like he needed one anyway. Boxing since he was twelve years old had given him a big head. He felt that he couldn't be beat.

James killed the car's engine and the loud music stopped instantaneously. By then, everyone else was already sliding out of the car. Mike didn't waste any time. He was already on his way over to talk to a group of females. Mike was the one who thought he was the real PrettyBoy out of the clique, always approaching women with no hesitation. He always felt that if you wanted it in life, you had to go get it. He was brown-skinned, medium built, 5'10", and wore his hair in braids. He looked kinda like he was mixed with Hispanic. But Mike never really could fuck with PrettyBoy in the looks department. James really considered himself as being a thug nigga, but he was a real pretty nigga, and that's why the nick name PrettyBoy stuck with him. He was light-skinned, 5'11", slim, and he wore four golds in his mouth. He kind of reminded you of a thug rendition of Goldy the Mac, and as he jumped out of the car, to the ladies, it was conspicuous. The first thing Pretty-Boy James did was look down at the new 24-inch chrome rims he had just put on his Chevy.

Damn, them muthafuckers hard, James thought to himself.

The first thing the ladies did was look at James. whispering, "Damn. That muthafucka fine!"

The crew made their way to the front of the club's entrance and Mike ran up to join them. They all were wearing black tonight, and it was for a reason. The crew had big ole plans for tonight - colossal plans.

When they got to the door where the bouncers stood, looking like two twin big black ugly gorillas, one stepped up like he thought the dudes were going to try to run inside the muthafucka.

"V.I.P.?" asked the bouncer, speaking to no one in particular

Mac spoke up. "Yeah, folk." He stepped up close enough to look up into the bouncer's eyes, then he pulled out a large bank roll and asked, "How much?"

That seemed to appease the bouncer as he cracked a smile. "Fifty dollars."

Mac then peeled off two one-hundred-dollar bills and handed them to the bouncer. The big black gorilla took the money, still smiling, and stepped back to pull the red rope, accommodating the crew with access to the club. He paid no attention to them all having on black. No one probably really noticed, because they all had on different styles of clothing. PrettyBoy had on Sean John jeans and a black T-shirt with a leather Sean John jacket. Mac wore an Akademik jogging suit. Mike had on an all-black Gucci suit. Jarvis wore a pair of Pelle Pelle black jeans, a black T-shirt with a Pelle Pelle jean jacket to match, and a black White Sox baseball cap. They all wore black Timberland boots.

They walked in S.D's feeling like they owned the muthafucka. The club was crunk. It was bumper to bumper, and they walked straight to the bar.

"What can I get y'all?" asked one of the bartenders

"Get me a bottle of Moet," responded PrettyBoy.

"Me too," followed Mac.

"Yeah, me too." agreed Jarvis, not wanting to miss the train.

"Fuck it, man, we might as well all get a bottle," said Mike with a handful of cash.

"Shit, how much they running for?" Jarvis asked.

"A hundred a bottle," said the bartender, looking hard.

"Damn," PrettyBoy said. "Man, work a nigga a deal since we all gettin' one." He was talking over the crowd and the exceedingly loud music.

"I'll tell you what," said the bartender. "If you all getting one, I'll change you 75 dollars apiece. I can't go no lower."

PrettyBoy pulled out his bankroll and said. "Give me six of them muthafuckas."

The bartender didn't waste time. He took the money and called over to some more bouncers and started to put Moet bottles on ice inside a big round bowl. The bouncers came behind the bar and the bartender said, "Take these guys up to VIP."

The bouncers grabbed the bowls on two trays and uttered, "Follow us."

They held the trays up in the air like waiters and walked right through the middle of the dance floor. The bouncers held flashlights in their hands and flashed them along the way as they yelled for everyone to move out of the way. They parted the crowd like the Red Sea. Some people had to stop dancing to let them by. The ladies were looking and trying to figure out who these niggas were. Once they walked through the dance floor, there was a flight of stairs right by the stage where guests performed. Another bouncer stood at the stairs in front of a red rope. They were meticulously escorted up. VIP was accommodated with Asian glass, tables, midnight black sofas, and sinking chairs. After the bouncers set the bowls down, they left.

The fellas all grabbed a bottle of Moet. There were champagne glasses all around the bowls, out lining the trays.

"I would like to propose a toast," said Mike as he popped a bottle.

"Yeah, yeah," all of them responded, ready to drink to whatever the occasion may be.

"To us," Mike finished over the Ying Yang's song "Get Low".

"To us!" everybody yelled back in harmony as they all busted out laughing.

That's when PrettyBoy spoke up. "My niggas, we gon' go down here and pull some of these hoes, get tipsy…but not too fucked up. It's going to be a long night. But enough of the small talk. Let's do this, Mac-11!"

They all yelled back, "Mac-11!"

The all-time classic hit from C-Murder, "Fuck Them Other Niggas", flooded the club speakers.

The Mac-11 crew went to shaking bottles up, letting champagne overflow. They began to turn up on a night that would surely make or break the Mac-11 crew once and for all.

Chapter 2
Mario and KeeKee

At about that same moment, in a white Escalade, KeeKee sat in the passenger seat listening to Jagged Edge on the SUV's system as it played low. She was staring out the window, seeming like her mind was in another place.

Mario was driving with one hand on the steering wheel while he slowly inhaled the smoke from the phat blunt of hydro weed he was smoking. He looked over at his girl KeeKee, checking out her impeccable body.

Damn, this hoe is fine, Mario thought. That's why he had been with her for two years now. His eyes looked down to her thighs. *Dark chocolate*. Mario licked his lips as he thought about pulling over and fucking her right then and there. It was his pussy. Shit, he knew he paid enough for it. KeeKee had expensive taste. Plus it didn't help that he let her know how much money he made from the dope games. Shit, the bitch was good as fuck helping him keep track of all the money he made. She even helped keep bookings and made sure his workers paid on time. All the weed Mario smoked, he would forget all types of shit, but KeeKee was very organized.

Mario was what they called hood rich. The last couple of years, he had been making over $40,000 a month. Money was good. One day, he believed he would be a millionaire for sure - if he could only just stop spending so much.

Mario was a major trick when it came to pussy. All the stripers loved to see him walk into the doors at Body Tap, Pleasers, Little Nikkie's, Magic City, The Gentlemen's Club…the list went on. He thought about the time he paid a stripper in New York five thousand dollars just to fuck her. He cracked a smile just thinking about the shit. *These hoes always think they getting over on a nigga*, Mario thought to himself. It really wasn't nothing to Mario. His motto was "It ain't tricking if you got it", and he lived by it. He had fucked some bad bitches, and it wasn't like Mario was the best-looking nigga in the ATL.

Matter of fact, he wasn't good-looking at all. He knew he was ugly, however, in the words of Biggie Smalls, "He stayed Coogi down to the socks". He knew that bitches loved money and would do whatever for it. Now for Mario's weakness with the ladies, he made up for with the niggas.

Niggas in the streets knew that Mario was no pushover, and the hoes did too, but the hoes tried him anyway. Rumors were that one nigga robbed him for five grand, but the outcome or result of this mistake was insurmountable. He found his mother and sister both dead at his apartment a couple of days later. Then, the nigga himself was found defunct a week later. It was said that Mario didn't use any of his workers for the hits. He did it himself. Not that he couldn't get someone to deal with the dilemma. A person could do a lot with money, and I believe we all know that.

"Damn, baby, I want some of that pussy," Mario said as KeeKee just kept staring out of the window, admiring the city lights. "Baby," Mario said louder, almost begging in his Keith Sweat voice.

"Huh? What?" KeeKee said. "Damn, what's up, baby?"

"You in another world?" Mario asked with his hand gripping his hard-on.

"Nall, baby, I'm just chillin'," KeeKee replied. "What was you sayin' now?" She asked, tryna regain focus.

"I was sayin', damn, baby, you wearin' the hell out of that dress," Mario replied, trying not to sound too thirsty.

Smiling, KeeKee asked, "Oh, you like this dress?" while slowly rubbing her hands up her thighs. Then she slowly slid her dress up until he could see that she wasn't wearing any panties. "Or do you like what's under this dress, baby?" KeeKee cooed while looking him in the eyes, with a look in her eyes like sex was the only thing on her mind.

Mario's eyes were locked in on her hairy box. He slowly licked his lips and said "Damn, baby, I think you right, it ain't the gotdamn dress!"

KeeKee smiled as if that pleased her. She knew how to please a man, and she definitely knew how to tease one too. She was elated that Mario had chosen to drive the truck, because if he would have driven one of his old schools with the sofa seat, he would have been all over her by now. She could remember a time when she really did like Mario.

16

He had done so much for her in the past, and even now, but when they first met is when he really did touch her heart.

KeeKee was an only child. Her mother was a conscientious woman and she did everything to spoil her daughter, giving her everything she wanted growing up. They stayed in a suburban area called Riverdale, about twenty minutes outside the city limits. But that didn't stop Kee-Kee from grinding her way to the hood. She only fucked with the ballers and street niggas. She didn't fuck with the 9-to-5 niggas – "the squares", she always joked.

It wasn't long before Diana realized that she had a wild daughter. Diana tried to stop her from having the older men popping up at her door at night, but punishing KeeKee only worked out for the worst, because while at work, KeeKee would do what the fuck she wanted to. But she had taken all that she could take when she caught KeeKee with her legs in the sky with a man, in her own damn bed, at the tender age of sixteen.

KeeKee was hot - real hot. When Diana walked in the room and saw what was going on after coming home early from work, Diana started yelling and screaming. She rushed the man and tried to pull him from her daughter, because he had to be raping her, so she thought. But to her surprise, KeeKee must have like it, because she jumped up and actually began to assail her mother. Diana was so surprised that she just stopped everything and stood there. She didn't even fight the girl back. While she was flabbergasted, the man ran out of the house, but the shock didn't last too long, because before Diana knew it, she was beating KeeKee's ass.

After that, she kicked KeeKee's hot ass out on the streets. Mario was the one that came to her rescue. From the first day, she never had to worry about anything. He was her knight in shining armor. But, now, that shit had worn off. She just didn't have nowhere else to go at the moment. But she was tired of faking it when they had sex.

Now that nigga she had been sleeping with for the last month…that was a man. *Damn, and he knows how to fuck*, thought KeeKee. She just couldn't get him off her mind. To KeeKee, it seemed like it would take Monday forever to get there.

Well, at least she would get to see him tonight at the club, even though they couldn't talk. *Damn, it's like a tease just to see him.* Thinking this, KeeKee pulled down her dress and said, "Calm down, daddy, we got all night." She flashed a Kool-Aid smile just before she started back looking out the window.

Tonight, she was in for some of her own medicine, because shit was about to go from 0-100 real quick.

Chapter 3
Club S.O.

Back at the Club S.O., PrettyBoy and his crew were making their way back down the stairs coming from the VIP room. Most of the ladies in the club were looking to see which one of them they thought was the flyest. The club was definitely jumpin'.

"I'm going to see how many of these hoes I can fuck tonight," Mike said, leaning over to PrettyBoy so he could hear him over the music.

"Put it down then," said PrettyBoy as they made their way through the crowded dance floor.

"Yeah shawty, you know they got a reggae dance floor downstairs," Jarvis told Mac as he turned up the bottle of Moe.

"Oh yeah?" said Jarvis. "Let's hit that muthafucka!"

"What's up?" said Mac presumptuously.

"Shit, nigga, let's ride," Jarvis said, as they both eased through the crowd.

Mike asked PrettyBoy, "What's up?"

"Shiitt, folk, I'll check it out later. I'm about to hit this bar right now, shawty," PrettyBoy answered, headed towards the bar.

"Let's ride," Mike said, on his heels, watching everything moving.

They both made their way to the bar, but right before they got there, PrettyBoy spotted something he liked and paused. She was brown-skinned, wore six-inch red-bottom heels, and some jeans that looked like they were painted on her. She looked about 5'9", 160 pounds, 34-24-38. She was thick. She wore a black top and a black cowboy hat.

There was another girl standing beside her and shawty was looking good too. She seemed to be about the same height, give or take an inch. She had on a red top that was showing her shoulders, plus she wore a black skirt. She was more on the slim side, but from behind she looked like she could be a model.

PrettyBoy couldn't tell from where he was standing, but once he stopped a few steps away from them, he hit Mike on the shoulder.

"What's up, my nigga? Let's jump down on them two hoes right there," PrettyBoy said with a slight head nod towards their victims.

Mike stopped and looked in their direction, then he cracked a smile when he saw the ladies looking right back at them. "Shiitt, you ain't said nothing," Mike answered confidently. Then he walked up to the one with the red shirt on and started a dialogue.

PrettyBoy stood there for a minute and stared at the brown-skinned stallion. They made eye contact and PrettyBoy locked in on her. The brown-skinned Goddess started to blush. That's when he knew that it was time for him to make his move. PrettyBoy took his time and walked over to her real slow, like he had forever and a day. He leaned over to her and whispered in her ear real soft. "What's the bizness, li'l mama? You want to come chill with me in VIP?" PrettyBoy asked, in his big daddy voice.

"That's cool," she said real sexy-like, topped off with a beautiful smile.

"What you drinking?" PrettyBoy asked before they left.

"Long Island Iced Tea," she answered, holding up her half empty cup.

PrettyBoy stepped over to the bar, a couple of feet from where they were standing, and asked for the drink. He then told the bartender to have him a bottle of Alize sent up to the VIP section. Then the four of them made their way up.

When they got there, they all sat at one of the tables. PrettyBoy was thinking to himself, *Damn that other broad had a phat ass after all.* But then he looked at the brown little dime piece he had sitting next to him and he couldn't complain. She was staring into PrettyBoy's eyes.

"What's your name, shawty?" asked PrettyBoy over the music.

"Jessica," she replied "What's your name?"

"They call me PrettyBoy," he said, all nonchalant

"Oh yeah?" Jessica said, smiling. She thought to herself, *I see why!*

"So where you from, Jessica?" he asked, making good convo.

"I'm from Miami, but I'm going to Spelman out here in Atlanta," answered Jessica, then she asked, "How old are you? You look kind of young." Jessica was in her senior year in college and was about to graduate this year.

Now it was PrettyBoy's turn to smile. "Oh yeah? Well. I'm legal, shawty," PrettyBoy said with a big smile.

This made Jessica laugh. "Boy you crazy, but that's cool," she said, taking a liking to PrettyBoy

They talked for a while and sipped their drinks.

Then the DJ yelled out, "This for my gangstas!" UGK's song "Murder" came on loud and clear.

Jessica and her friend jumped up, saying, "This that shit right here! Hell yeah, girl!" Then both of them started to bounce their asses in Mike's and PrettyBoy's faces.

Both of the fellas looked at each other.

Mike yelled, with a smile on his face, "Oh shit, I might have myself a gangsta bitch!" He lifted the blunt in his hand up into the air and bounced to the music.

PrettyBoy pulled out the weed he brought into the club and started to roll a blunt. All the while, he was looking at Jessica's phat ass as it bounced up and down. *Now that's a phat ass*, he thought to himself as he sat back into the seat and fired up his blunt, enjoying the view.

Trai'Quan

Chapter 4
Where the plug at???

Mario walked into the club with his girl KeeKee right beside him. They walked over to the bar and KeeKee sat on one of the bar stools as Mario stood beside her and ordered himself a double shot of Hen on ice. He looked over to KeeKee and asked, "Baby, what you want?"

"Get me an Incredible Hulk," she replied, needing something strong. The drink was Hypnotic and Hennessy mixed together.

Mario gave the bartender their order, then turned around to check out the crowd. He saw a few good-looking ladies in the club. He knew he couldn't fuck with them tonight though - not with KeeKee with him. *The bitch would have a fit*, Mario thought, visualizing the disaster before it happened.

He remembered the time she had thought he was fucking the girl that stayed next door. She knocked on the door until she answered and hit the bitch right in the mouth. Mario hadn't even fucked the girl, but he had got some head. He liked the fact that she would fight for him. Plus, he did care about KeeKee in a major way. Hell, he thought that he might even love her. He figured that she knew about his flings here and there, but he knew that she needed him. Who else would take care of her like he did? Sometimes he felt that she thought he would leave her. He deduced that was probably part of the reason why she didn't want him going back and forth to New York on the frequent trips he made.

That was why they were here tonight in Club S.O.'s. He had told his connect (plug) in New York that he needed it to be brought down to the A-Town from now on. It would cost him extra, but what the fuck did he care? Twenty keys of cocaine had to be driven all the way from New York, so he didn't mind remunerating extra to take away some of the risk. Hell, he was tired of getting them bitches to make the trip while he tailed them in another car. He knew the feds would give a nigga 50 years if they ever caught him or if one of them hoes were to turn state. So it was all good. KeeKee was good for him.

Mario looked around to see if he could spot his New York connect anywhere in the spot. He checked his watch. "Damn, baby, them niggas ain't even here yet," he said to KeeKee, like she was his business manager or sum.

She looked up, holding her drink in one hand, while she played with the straw in her drink with the other and replied, "They'll probably be here in a minute."

"Yeah," Mario mumbled, still looking around.

"You know they got a reggae floor downstairs," she said, tryna get his mind off of the mission at hand.

"Oh yeah?" Mario said. "Well look, I'm about go see if I see them niggas."

"You want me to come with you?" KeeKee asked.

"Nall, baby girl, just chill. You just sit there and look pretty, I'll be back," Mario responded before taking his drink from the bar and walking off.

As soon as Mario walked away, KeeKee began to scan the club with her eyes, like she was looking for someone…in hopes of seeing him…

Chapter 5
Sexy

Just then, PrettyBoy James was on his way down from the VIP section. *Damn*, he thought to himself. The VIP room was off the chain. There were so many hoes up there. It seemed that they had the club on lock-down for all the hoes that were on the dance floor.

Mike really showed his ass tonight. That nigga something else, thought PrettyBoy.

He had surprised him as much as he did Jessica and her friend when he got up and left, then came back five minutes later with two light-skinned broads, holding each of their hands. And when he sat down across from them, he sat one in his lap and the other one in the chair beside him. Jessica's friend looked like she was about to cry. PrettyBoy couldn't help but to laugh just thinking about the shit.

Mac had brought a whole click of hoes with him back from the reggae floor. The VIP was packed now. PrettyBoy was on his way to see what was up with the reggae floor. Then he thought about it, and decided to hit the bar first to get a Corona.

As he made his way to the bar, walking through the crowd, he saw her, dark chocolate. She wore her long black hair pulled back into a ponytail going down to her back. She had Chinese eyes, and her body was to kill for. She wore a black dress that didn't want it, black boots to match and shawty was blinged out. Diamonds were on her neck, wrist, finger, and ears.

***

KeeKee noticed him as soon as he came down the stairs from the VIP section. *Damn, that nigga looking good tonight*, was all she could think. She didn't see him with anybody, no female with him. Now that was a good thing. Now this nigga wasn't no Mario, that's for sure, and he probably had bitches throwing their panties at him. *Now this is a real man*, KeeKee thought while she sat there, playing with the straw in her drink. She ogled him as he made his way through the crowd coming right towards her. "Damn, don't come talk to me, please don't come talk to me!" she said to herself as he approached. She was glad Mario had walked off because she didn't think she would've been able to maintain her composure. Mario probably would have seen something in her eyes or he would have witnessed the way that she was acting, squirming all around in her seat and all. Mario wasn't slow, she knew that fo' sho'. He could pick up on shit like that especially when it came to niggas, because he was over protective about her. Well, at least that's what KeeKee liked to think.

Damn, she thought. *Well, here goes nothing*, as PrettyBoy walked right past KeeKee, about three stools over from her where this big girl was sitting at the bar, looking like "Hey Kool-Aid". Everything she wore was red, even her lipstick. PrettyBoy leaned into the bar and ordered a Corona. He acted as if he didn't even see KeeKee. When the bartender handed him his drink, he took the beer and gave the big girl a smile, looking over at KeeKee. He took a sip from his beer and walked off.

Damn, the nigga smooth too, KeeKee thought as she watched him walking off, disappearing back into the crowd.

Her drink sat in her hand. She no longer played with her straw as she thought to herself, *That nigga know he sexy!*

Chapter 6
It's showtime

PrettyBoy was on his way down the stairs when he walked past Mario, who was on his way up with two dudes that looked like they could be from New York. He could tell just from their style. The men didn't say anything when they walked past each other, but they did lock eyes for a succinct second.

The reggae section wasn't as packed, but there was enough weed smoke in the air to make you think that you were in Jamaica. The DJ spun Shyne's song, "Bad Boys". PrettyBoy walked through the floor until he saw Jarvis. He was sitting over in a corner smoking a blunt. A girl sat beside him, and another one danced to the music slowly and seductively in front of him. As PrettyBoy walked over to him, Jarvis yelled over the music, "What's the bizness, rude boy?" in his Jamaican accent.

"Let's go, shawty, it's time to handle bizness," PrettyBoy replied vivaciously.

Jarvis stood up and pushed the girl that was in front of him out of the way.

"Gotdamn, nigga!" she yelled, tryna catch her balance, almost falling on her face.

He paid her no attention as he walked off with PrettyBoy. They went to get Mac and Mike from the VIP and while up there, Jessica stopped PrettyBoy.

"What's up ,baby?" asked PrettyBoy.

"You leaving already? The night is still young" she asked, really wanting to spend more time with him.

"Yeah, baby girl, but I'm going to get up with you later though," he assured her as he made his exodus.

"Well, you got my number, nigga, you better use it!" she shot back. PrettyBoy smiled.

"Yeah, I'm gon' do that," he said before walking off.

The fellas all walked out of the club, passing the bar, passing right by Mario, the two New Yorkers, and KeeKee. No one really paid them any attention – well, no one except for KeeKee, that is…

***

"Mario," stated Mouse, one of the New Yorkers. He got the name because he had a voice like Mike Tyson. The other New Yorker was GridLock. No one really know how he got his nickname, but everyone in his hood in Brooklyn, NY knew he a mean muthafucka and was nothing to play with. He was about 250 pounds. Just from his look, one would guess that he had seen a hard time in the penitentiary. He had tattoos all over his body and face.

"So everything's everything, right, God?" Mouse continued on.

That was his way of asking did Mario have the money with him for the 20 keys of cocaine that they had in the truck outside.

"Yeah, folk, everything's good, my nigga," Mario said to Mouse as they killed the small talk in the club.

"So what the fuck are we waiting on? Yo, let's get this shit over with!" GridLock spoke up, eager to seal the deal and get back to the Big Apple.

"Let's do this," Mario said. He told KeeKee, "Let's ride, baby, it's showtime."

Chapter 7
The parking lot

As soon as PrettyBoy and his crew got outside, they moved with great velocity. Everybody got in the car except PrettyBoy. He went straight to the trunk and pulled out two Mac-11 machine guns and a black plastic bag. Then he jumped in the driver's seat. He gave Mac and Jarvis each a Mac-11 and handed everyone a black ski mask from the bag. Everybody in the car put the ski masks on their heads, but didn't pull them all the way down.

"Y'all ready to do this shit?" PrettyBoy asked while he pulled his .45 from under the seat.

"Hell yeah," answered Jarvis instantly.

"All the time," shot Mac, checking the machine gun in his hand to make sure that there was one in the chamber.

"You only live once, so why not?" said Mike, clicking back his .45, making the hammer stay back.

PrettyBoy broke his machination down to his crew. "Okay, check this out. I don't know what car the New York niggas came in, plus they may have someone in the parking lot in another car watching, or watching from somewhere else, so everybody keep your eyes open. Now that's Mario's truck right there. We'll wait to see where everybody goes, but he gots to have the 200 thou in the truck. Jarvis, me and you take the nigga Mario, but you stand back and watch the lot too. I should handle him with no problem. You just watch my back, shawty, and everybody else's too. You got me?" asked PrettyBoy, amped up and ready to handle business.

"My nigga, you know I'm going to hold you down," Jarvis said with the Mac in his hand, as he listened to the plan.

"Mike, you and Mac take them New York niggas. Both of y'all play them real close. I don't like the look of that big one with all them tats. It's a big play going down, y'all. Let's get this money," PrettyBoy finished, allowing everyone to get their minds right.

"It's showtime," Mike said, spotting Mario's entourage coming out of the club.

Mario and KeeKee walked over to the Escalade. KeeKee got in on the passenger side. Mario got in for a few seconds, then got back out of the truck and went to the back, where he began to open the truck's back door. The New Yorkers went to a black Suburban parked on the other corner of the parking lot.

"Let's do it!" PrettyBoy said.

They all pulled their ski masks down and jumped out of the car.

Mario heard the noise of the car doors opening up then turned to see what was going on, but by the time he saw the two men in masks walking up with guns, he knew it was too late to pull for his shit.

"Whoa, whoa, what's up, folk?" Mario said, lifting his hands to the sky, tryna play it off.

Before he knew it, he was hit square in the face with PrettyBoy's pistol. Mario dropped to one knee, yelling while blood cascaded from his nose like water from a fountain.

"Shut the fuck up!" PrettyBoy said, grabbing him by his shirt, lifting him to his feet. Then he lifted Mario's shirt and took the gun that was tucked in his waist. It was a chrome Desert Eagle. After he was finish searching Mario, he looked in the back of the truck and his eyes lit up when he saw a black briefcase.

When KeeKee saw what was going down as she sat in the passenger seat of the truck looking out through the back, she couldn't help but to scream.

"Oh my God, oh shit!" She saw men with masks on their face, giving her boyfriend Mario the business.

Mac and Mike both caught the two New Yorkers at the back of the Suburban just opening the two back doors of the truck. GridLock felt the pistol to his head first.

"Don't move, bitch, or I'll blow your muthafuckin' brains out," Mike said to the big New Yorker.

At the same time, Mac told the other one, "Now you step back two steps."

Mouse did exactly what he was told.

"Now turn your punk ass around," Mac said belligerently and Mouse did it.

"Now step about five paces to the left," Mac commanded.

Then he watched Mouse closely as he did just that

Now it was Mike's turn to give some orders. "Now you reach in the truck and give me that duffle bag."

GridLock reached in the truck, pulled out the duffle bag, and turned around to face the two robbers. Mike still held the .45 to his head. He took the bag, wrapped it around his shoulder, and then he told both men, "Lift up y'all muthafuckin' shirts and turn around slow."

They did, and Mike took Mouse's gun first, a .38 revolver. Then he took the gun GridLock had in the small of his back, which was a Glock 40. Then they told both men to lay on the ground. Just as Grid-Lock and Mouse fell to their knees, shots rang out from inside the Suburban. The dude that was inside the suburban laying on the back seat sat up and went to dumping rounds at Mac and Mike. In return, both started to empty their clips as they moved for cover. Mac's Mac-11 bullets ripped through the Suburban, breaking windows and putting holes in the interior.

Mike ran sideways while dumping rounds at the Suburban. Someone's bullet caught the guy inside the truck right in the forehead, but not without Mike catching a bullet himself in the shoulder, causing him to fall to the ground. Mac saw this and turned his gun on Mouse and let loose about six shots right to his chest while he was trying to get up from the ground.

GridLock was trying to crawl under a nearby car. Mac released more shots at him, leaving holes in the side of the car. GridLock rolled underneath, not knowing if he was hit or not.

***

When PrettyBoy and Jarvis heard the gunshots, they knew something was erroneous. They didn't waste any time. PrettyBoy snatched the briefcase filled with money, and Jarvis ran to see what had happened. PrettyBoy turned to face Mario with his gun in one hand and the briefcase in the other. Mario must have seen it coming, because he put his hands in the sky and began to beg.

"Man, don't shoot me, please don't shoot me!"

But PrettyBoy wasn't listening. He let go four shots into Mario's chest. Then PrettyBoy looked up and caught eyes with KeeKee, who was looking back at the whole thing. She didn't look too surprised; she just stared into his eyes. PrettyBoy broke the gaze, then ran off with the briefcase in his hand. He had to see what was up with his partners, and they had to get the hell out of here and fast.

Jarvis made it over to the side of the parking lot where it was going down at, and the scene didn't look pretty. He saw Mike laying on the ground as he ran up head first with the Mac-11 machine gun in his hand. He ran over to Mike and grabbed him.

"You alright, shawty?" Jarvis yelled at the top of his lungs.

"Ahh, huh, uhhhh, I'm hit, my nigga. Ah shit, the muthafucka shot me," Mike forced the words out his mouth.

"Come on, we got to get to the car before the police come!" Jarvis yelled to Mike. He could already hear the police sirens in the distance. He helped Mike stand, threw his arm around him and they made their way to the car.

Mac followed them, walking backward as PrettyBoy met them at the car. Seconds later, you could hear the sound of tires skid off.

Chapter 8
Back ready and steady
A few weeks later

In Decatur, GA on Westly Chapel Road, the streets were exceedingly busy. They were always busy, two lanes up and down with nonstop traffic. All of the popular fast food restaurants were up and down the strip along with hotels, gas stations, and there was even a movie theater and a few clubs located on this popular street.

In an apartment complex named Lantana that sat right off of the busy street, inside of the townhome style apartment 1213, the lights were on, the blunt smoke was in the air, and bottles were also being popped. PrettyBoy stood at the head of the table. He wore white and blue swim trunks by Sean John, a white Sean John wife beater with some Prada slip-n-slide in sandals, and a blue and white Royals baseball cap with a strap on the back to adjust it. He wore a diamond necklace that hung to his belly button, a diamond watch, bracelet, and ring. He was draped in diamonds. Beside him sat a beautiful young woman who went by the name of KeeKee. She sat in a chair close to him at the corner of the dining room table. She looked sexy in her blue Prada bikini top with the bottom of the swimsuit covered up with a white and blue scarf rapped around her waist. She was blinged out like always. She also had on open toe heels to match and her hair was pulled back into a ponytail like Pocahontas with rings around the ponytail, kind of like a Native American woman. She had a glow in her eyes and smile on her face.

To her left sat Mac. He had a towel draped over his shoulders over his wife beater and a pair of red and cream trunks with a creme Atlanta Braves fitted cap. A cigar filled with weed was hanging from his mouth as he sat back, taking a pull from the blunt. He was also blinged out and wore all Sean John.

Across the table from him sat Jarvis. He had a black White Sox baseball cap on backwards, a dark green short sleeve button down shirt and shorts to match, and a pair of black sandals, all Stacey Adams. His shirt hung open to show his long platinum chain filled with diamonds. He also wore a diamond ring and watch. He was iced out.

Next to him sat Monica. They all had grown up together on the westside streets of Atlanta. Monica was about 5'8", brown skin, 165. She was in excellent shape from her time spent in the penitentiary. She had done a two-year bid for possession of crack cocaine and attempt to distribute. It was her second time getting caught. She was older than the fellas by a year and some change, but ever since she had come home, she had been with them nonstop. You wouldn't have been able to tell that Monica had done time if you didn't know her story. The girl was fine, a dime piece, a real badass bitch with a cute face and perfect ass. The niggas in the streets loved her fat ass and pretty face, but if you looked deep into her eyes, you could tell that the girl was dangerous. She had juicy lips, a small button nose, and she kept her shit together. Only the best could go on her 32-21-38 frame. Tonight, she wore gold big earrings, a small gold chain, a big gold bracelet, a Chanel top with the sleeves cut off with a wide neckline on the top, teasing you with a shot of cleavage. The shirt was white, orange, and red. Her white Chanel pants that stopped at her calf went well with her open toe sandals.

Down at the other end of the table sat with his shirt off sat Mike with a bandage over his shoulder where he had been shot. This time he wasn't just showing off his tattoos. His Atlanta Braves baseball cap was tilted to one side of his head. His arm was in a sling. He wore blue jean Enyce shorts with all white Nike Air Max. He sat there sipping out a bottle of VSOP Remy Martin. They had weed all over the table, a box of 50 Optimo blunts, bottles of liquor, Hennessy Black, Moet, and Remy.

"Nigga, your ass almost got left by the ship. If it wasn't for me, your ass would be in Montego Bay calling collect, muthafucka," PrettyBoy joked.

"Shitting me," Mike joked back. "I would have swam my black ass back, or them crazy-ass Jamaican women would have fucked me to death!"

They all had to laugh at that one. They were all feeling good from the cruise they had taken to Jamaica. It was three extravagant days, and they had just gotten back. Mike had still been chasing all the ladies, with a hurt shoulder and all.

"You a fool, boy," Jarvis spoke up "I thought that hoe was going to kill you the way she was riding your dick. Man, y'all woke me up the way both of y'all was hollering," Jarvis said, joking with Mike. "My nigga, I'm talking about you over there like, 'oh, oh, oooohhhh shit, oh shit, oh shit.' " Everybody started laughing as Jarvis kept going. "Gotdamn, playboy!"

"Shit, the bitch kept touching my gotdamn shoulder," Mike said through laughter as they all laughed even more. "Oh, now don't front, nigga, your ass didn't mind walking over to the bed to get some head," Mike finished talking and then gave Jarvis a smile.

Everybody knew that Monica and Jarvis had been fucking on the low for a while now. Neither one of them were faithful. They just did they thing for the sex. So when Mike said this, it caused a lot of laughter in the house. Monica fixed Jarvis with a mean stare, while she reached over and hit him on the arm, a playful lick saying "you ain't shit nigga," all the while cracking a smile.

Jarvis smiled and started laughing. "What?" he said, throwing his hands up to block more blows from landing. "I must have been sleep-walking, baby." This caused more laughter and Monica couldn't help but to burst out laughing herself.

"Oh hell nall, with your crazy ass," she said, then she hit him again.

They laughed and started to come down a little. As the laughter died, PrettyBoy spoke up. "That shit was epic. We going to have to do that again"

"Fo' sho'," replied Mac, already thirsty to go back.

"Yeah, we definitely going to have to take another cruise," agreed Monica as she took a sip from her cup.

"Yeah, next time we got to do a seven-day cruise," Mike insisted as they all were truly looking forward to a future of longevity.

Jarvis said, "Yeah, one of them ones for couples or something like that."

"Oh hell nall," said Mike. "Now you trippin'."

They laughed a little more, enjoying each other's company.

"Nall, next time we go somewhere where there's a cabin and snow and shit like that."

Mac shot in there real quick, taking it to another level. "Yeah, we can rent a cabin next time, that shit sound real fly."

PrettyBoy said, "But y'all check this out. Right now, I would like to propose a toast." Everybody grabbed their glasses. Once they all had glasses in their hands, PrettyBoy spoke. "This toast is for Mike," he said, looking at his childhood friend from across the table. He went on, "I'm glad that the bullet went straight through and our man is in good shape, plus you know real niggas don't die," PrettyBoy stated cracking a smile.

Mike gave a little laugh and everybody else did too.

"Yeah, fo' sho'," Mac said.

"Okay," followed up Monica with a colossal smile

"Believe it," continued Jarvis with his cup in the air

"All the time, baby," finished Mike. He was glad to be alive after that slug.

Then PrettyBoy went on, "I know we all feel the same way, because without you, my nigga, there ain't no Mac-11 clique. We all links to the chain,"

"And KeeKee, baby," he said, turning to face her, "without you, none of this would have been possible. It's us until the end of time, baby. This toast is to us." He looked at everyone slowly and went on, "To all of us, to family. Mac-11!"

Everybody lifted their glasses and toasted. "Mac-11!" they all yelled in unison.

Chapter 9
Better learn, you fuckin' fool!
Da Bluff

On the other side of town, on the westside of Atlanta, was a hood called "The Bluff", a hood notoriously known for its heroin traps, where the junkies walked the streets like zombies day and night. It was another world. The young teenage blacks stood outside, selling every kind of drug you could imagine. People getting robbed and murdered was something everyone had gotten used to. Kids as young as fourteen years old packed pistols under their shirts. This was the streets in full effect. This neighborhood had earned the nickname "better leave, you fuckin' fool", and this title gave everyone that wasn't 'bout their issue the best advice that they could ever receive: just leave.

At a rundown house in the heart of The Bluff, burglar bars were on the doors and windows. Inside the house was GridLock and a few of his homies from New York. This was one of the many crack houses that was on the drug-infested block. Guns lay all over the house, everything from AK-47s to 12-gauge pumps, Glock 9s, Tec's, and revolvers. You had to be known in this part of town for the robbers and cops. There were about 11 people in the house with GridLock as he sat at the kitchen table. It was a small old wooden table, made in the shape of a circle. Drugs and guns covered the table. He held a blunt in his hand as he spoke.

"Yo son, I'm telling you, I want these muthafuckas toed up and duck taped. I'm going to kill each one by beating them in the fucking head with a fucking hammer."

He spoke with malice and tears in his eyes. One dude was sitting at the table with him while three more stood around the table listening. The rest of the people in the house were busy making crack sales and other jobs that they were allocated to perform. The man that sat at the table with GridLock was a black ugly muthafucka with a long scar on his face. He looked Haitian. He went by the nickname of Snake. GridLock looked him right in the eyes and went on.

"Them niggas killed Mouse. It ain't even about the fucking money. I will not sleep until these muthafuckas got tags on they toes. I want the ones who pulled the trigger, their mothers, their sisters, their fucking kids, son, we ain't going to play with these niggas!" GridLock said, hitting the table with murder in his eyes.

"What do you want me to do about Mario?" Snake asked, ready to get his hands dirty.

"Bring him to me. We going to get some answers from that muthafucka," GridLock said while taking a pull from the blunt he held in his hand, then he blew out the smoke exceedingly hard. "Then we going to kill the bitch."

GridLock and Snake were in sad remembrance that Mario had to shake his head for the loss of Mouse, as both New Yorkers anticipated their next move. Snake looked at his homie with the screw face/Johnny Blaze impression, responding, "It would be my pleasure to lend my skills and services too."

They both hopped and went out on the search like Google.

***

Back at the spot in Lantana (Decatur, GA), PrettyBoy sat down and went to hollering at his crew.

"All right, check this out, down to business. We got 20 keys of some good shit. That's the good part. But the problem is we only got one spot to move the shit out of in Cobb County, Six Flags Drive. We have already been making about four thousand a day out of there. Now I know we should be able to double that number. Now we could take the bricks and sell them in weight." He paused to see how that was going across. "But I don't want to do that. I want to grind this shit out and stack every dime, nickel, and penny we can get," informed Pretty-Boy as he brought to their attention what needed to be discussed.

"Fo' sho', my nigga. That's what time it is," Mike shot quickly, making his thoughts known to the crew.

PrettyBoy carried on. "This what we can do. I want to open up spots on Bankhead Highway, Hollywood Road, Cascade, Riverdale, and College Park. You know what I'm saying?" He glanced around at all of those present. "I want to move in on all the surrounding counties around Atlanta: Dekalb, Clayton, Gwinnett, and Douglas. I'm talking about taking over blocks. If niggas don't like us moving in, then they can move out. This way we get way more money out of this shit. And we make this Mac-11 shit more colossal than life itself," PrettyBoy said with passion in his eyes.

"I'm feeling that shit, PrettyBoy. We can do this," Monica said.

"I'm saying though. Y'all, that's a lot of spots we talking about. You sure we going to have enough work and money to really do it like that?" Jarvis asked.

"We all straight from the $200,000 we split. So we can wait to see the money come back from this thing. Because it's going to take time, but when it do start to flow, my nigga, it's going to rain," PrettyBoy bragged. He took the time to glance over at Mac while still carrying on. "You'll be over recruiting. You already got your li'l brother and all his partners and them. Plus I'm going to need you or Jarvis to holla at y'all uncle Big Nard on that gun contact he got in Tennessee so we can get strapped."

"I got you, my nigga. I'm ready to do this thang," Mac responded.

"Monica, you'll be over real estate. I need you to be over getting us a spot to put it down in every county," PrettyBoy said. He thought about it a moment. "Look around for spots where people might not notice the traffic. Spots where it's already being drugs sold at and seem to be making good money. We'll make our shit so good, we'll take their clientele. As far as the spots that don't have no junkies there, don't worry. We'll make it so sweet for them - the prices, the size - our shops will never close.

"Alright, that's a bet." Monica replied.

"Jarvis," PrettyBoy said while looking at him.

"Yeah, what's up?" Jarvis responded.

"Look, what I need you to do is be the pick-up man. Once everything rolling smooth, I'm going to need you to hit all the spots and make sure the intake is straight. I'll work all of the numbers out later. Just do this for me," PrettyBoy said.

Trai'Quan

Chapter 10
Just a little bit

Mario was sitting on the passenger side of his partner Tec's Range Rover. Earlier that day he had just been let out of Grady Memorial Hospital. He leaned back in the seat of the Range Rover while T.I's new song played on the radio, "Stand Up". He listened to the music while he rode and tried to let everything that had happened soak into his mind. Mario stared out of the window all he could think of was KeeKee.

Something was definitely up with shawty, he thought to himself. Then Tec said something, breaking his concentration at the moment.

"Mario, you alright, shawty?" Tec asked.

"Yeah, I'm straight, my nigga," he said while still thinking. But then he glanced over at Tec. "My nigga, I just can't believe that some niggas caught me slippin' like that. Man, it's like they already knew the move was going down. Shit, they had to!" Mario started shaking his head, tryna figure this mess out.

"You think them New York niggas set you up?" asked Tec, tryna help his partner compile clues, theories, or even and assumption.

"Nall, it couldn't have been a set up because two of them niggas got killed," Mario responded with frustration written all over his face, yet still he went on talking. "It's only one other person that knew about that deal going down that night other than me."

"Who?" Tec asked with anticipation that could've lasted a lifetime.

"Man...KeeKee," Mario concluded like she was really the last person in the world that he wanted it to be. She had been coming to see him every day at the hospital, by his side like the perfect woman - well, all the way up until a couple of days ago when she said that she needed a break, that she was tired of seeing him like that and that she just wanted him to get out and come home. He told her that it was cool for her to take a break. The doctor had said that he'd be able to leave and go home in a couple of days so for about four days, he hadn't seen or heard from her. He figured that she needed some time for herself, but once he got alone and had time to think, his brain went into work overtime. He knew it had to be that bitch KeeKee.

"You think that hoe set you up?" Tec asked, looking at his friend, eager for his answer. Tec was Mario's protégé. He was only twenty years old. Mario had him by nine years. He was also in the dope game, but he didn't have as much money as Mario. He had been down with Mario since he was sixteen years old. They had major love for each other, and Tec would put a bullet in anybody's head for his big homie. It pissed him off to even think of a bitch setting his partner up. Now Tec was different from his friend when it came to females. He fucked a lot of bitches, but he didn't pay for it. His motto was "all I got for a bitch is dick and bubbled bum, and I'm all out of bubble gum." He wasn't the prettiest nigga in the world, but he wasn't ugly either. He was 6'2" ,180 pounds, with brown skin. He kind of looked like the rapper Method Man. Tec had on a brown and black outfit with a matching hat and a pair of gray and black Timberland boots. He was looking at Mario, waiting for his response.

"Yeah, man, it had to be that hoe," Mario deduced with belligerence in his voice and eyes.

"Well, we gon' have to deal with this shit, get to the bottom of it. I'll take care of that bitch," Tec continued, looking at his big homie.

"Nall, folk, we gon' do this shit together," Mario said while rubbing his stomach where the shit bag was. He had to wear it for a couple of months, the doctor had told him. "We going to handle this shit tonight!"

"So how you want to do it?" Tec asked.

"We just going to go to my spot, get this bitch, and take her somewhere that nobody won't hear her muthafuckin' ass scream, and then we going to get some answers out this hoe!" Mario yelled, pausing for a minute. He went on to say, "Then we gon' leave that punk-ass bitch stankin'!"

Tec shook his head as though he was truly satisfied, ready to perform the mission and annihilation at hand.

Chapter 11
Finally by ourselves!

In Decatur, everybody was leaving the house. They gave each other pounds and hugs. Monica and Jarvis left first.

"Alright, y'all, we out," Monica informed, grabbin' her purse off the living room table as she bounced.

Everybody was kicking it in the living room now. They had the entertainment system going. PrettyBoy was sitting on the big sofa with KeeKee under his arm.

"Alright, girl, y'all be easy," KeeKee replied back.

"Don't forget to call me," Monica told her.

"Alright, I won't."

"Bye," KeeKee said as Monica walked out the door. Jarvis stood at the door. "I'm going to hit you up on your cell in the morning," he told PrettyBoy.

"Alright, that's a bet," he agreed before Jarvis walked out of the house, closing the door behind him.

Mac was sitting in the lounge chair, talking on his cell phone with some hoes. They were talking freaky as he stood up. "Man, look, I'm going to get up with y'all niggas. I got something I need to go handle," he said, walking towards the door.

"You sure you don't need no help with that, playboy?" Mike asked Mac before he walked out the house, paying him no attention at all.

"Nall, partner, this some straight solo action right here." Mac smiled as he ambled out.

"Man, hold up!" Mike yelled, running out, following him.

PrettyBoy and KeeKee started to laugh.

They laughed and looked into each other's eyes. Slowly, they stopped laughing and both of them had smiles on their faces. They could feel the heat that their bodies were giving off. Neither one of them tried to hide the hunger and desire in their eyes. PrettyBoy got up to close the door of the house. He looked out and saw Mike and Mac both getting in Mac's '79 Buick Cutlass. *Yes!* he thought to himself, as he closed the door. He looked over at KeeKee and said, "Finally, just me and you."

KeeKee smiled at him as he walked over to the entertainment system.

"Let's get some real music in this muthafucka, something we can groove to," he said as he hit a few buttons. Ginuwine came on the stereo: "My whole life has changed"/

"Okay. That's what I'm talking about," KeeKee said while she was getting up from the sofa. She made her way over to him.

He grabbed her into his arms and they sway to the music. "Baby, you made my whole life change, for real," PrettyBoy whispered into her ear.

"I wish that we could stay like this forever," KeeKee said as she put her head on his shoulder. "Baby, why don't you change my life too?"

"What you mean, baby?" He was confused

"I don't want to go back to him, PrettyBoy. I want to stay with you. I did everything just like you told me to. Now I'm tired of playing this game. I want to be with you and only you," she told him truthfully.

PrettyBoy looked into her eyes. "You ain't never got to go back, baby. I don't want you to go nowhere but in my arms," he said as he kissed her. They kissed long and hard.

When they came up for air, KeeKee said, "I love you."

PrettyBoy looked at her and looked deep into her eyes. "Baby, I love you too."

They kissed and didn't stop as his hand slowly made its way from the small of her back to the round shape of her ass. He gripped it, filling both of his hands up.

KeeKee let out a gasp. "Uhhhh!"

He moved his mouth from her lips and went down to her neck. He used his tongue like a snake, rubbing it across her throat.

"Oooohhhh," she moaned as he took one of his hands from her behind and started to caress her breasts, slowly massaging her nipples through her shirt.

She rubbed on his chest. He started to unbutton her jeans, then slipped one hand inside until he felt her bush, then he found the wet spot that he was looking for. He placed one finger inside of her, pushing it in and out, in and out, in and out.

"Ooohhh, baby," KeeKee moaned, "go ahead and fuck me, just fuck me!" she screamed tensely.

He undressed her while she undressed him. In seconds they both were naked as they went to the stairs, but before they could make their way up, they ended up on the stairs making love. She was on her knees doggy style and he was giving her the business. Straight pain accompanied pleasure. She could feel every thrust as he rammed his dick inside of her wet pussy hole, harder and harder each time.

"Oh shit!" she moaned over his hard breathing. "It feels so good."

He pushed deeper inside of her wetness. "Oh, you like that?" he asked as he thrust inside her harder. "You like that?"

"Yeeeeessssss! Yeesss, daddy, yessss!" she screamed, resting her head on the stairs, allowing her goodness to flood, grip, and lock on the cock.

He put his hand in between her legs and felt for her clit until he found it. He began to play with it, gentle and meticulously.

"Uhhhh," she moaned as she bit down on her lip.

He could feel his hand soaking wet from her juices. He pushed inside her, then stopped and stayed inside her as deep as he could go. Then he took her long ponytail in his hand. He pulled back on it slowly, gently, and seductively.

"Come on, you coming with me. Get up." He watched her slowly get to her feet with him still inside of her. It made his dick throb even more.

KeeKee slowly lifted her head up from the stairs as she stood to her feet. They walked like that to the sofa, then she laid on her stomach. He stayed on top of her, letting his dick go in and out of her wet vagina.

"Oooohhhh, baby!" she yelled as she climaxed on the dick.

"Damn, baby," he said then he came deep inside of her warm juice box, exceedingly exhausted as they both lay there in ecstasy.

Trai'Quan

Chapter 12
We gotta find some!

At Mario's house on Cascade Road, the lights were off, but there was abundant activity going on inside. The house was big, white, and lavish, almost like a mini mansion. It was one of those big white houses you saw in the movies

Snake and his crew were in the house fucking everything up. He wanted Mario to know that they had been there, plus he was looking for money and drugs.

"This nigga got to have a spot where he keep all his bread at!" Snake said under his breath while flipping over the mattress in the main bedroom. He took a knife from his pocket and cut the mattress open. He looked inside. "Not in there," he said, putting the knife back in his pocket, making his way to the dresser.

As he was yanking the drawers out, one of his boys called him from another room. "Snake!"

"Jackpot!" Snake yelled out loud, walking towards the room his homeboy was calling from.

It was a safe. The safe was built inside of the room's closet. It was behind a fake wall that was supposed to fool the naked eye, but luckily Snake's homeboy had busted a hole straight through the muthafucka. They all stared through the hole at the big safe.

"What the fuck y'all waiting on?" Snake asked the other three dudes standing in the room. "Break this muthafuckin' wall down!" Then he kicked his foot straight through the wall, finding the surprise of a lifetime...

Trai'Quan

Chapter 13
Better safe than sorry!

KeeKee rolled over in bed with PrettyBoy as they had finally made it to the bedroom. "Whoooo!" KeeKee cooed, still tryin' to catch her breath.

They both were breathing hard from another round of hot steamy sex.

"Damn, baby, you going to kill a bitch," she proclaimed smiling with the sheets pulled up to her chest.

"Shit, you the murderer!" he shot back as they smiled at each other.

PrettyBoy sat up in bed, reached over, and grabbed a blunt from the nightstand. Then he opened one of the drawers and came out with a bag of weed. KeeKee saw the color of the weed in the bag and thought that her eyes were playing tricks on her.

"Baby, that shit looks black. You going to smoke that?"

"Hell yeah, this that purple. This going to have you fucked up."

"Oh shit, well hurry up and tie that shit up," she said as she watched him rolling up the blunt.

PrettyBoy laughed. When he finished rolling the blunt, they laid in the bed, passing it back and forth, taking pulls.

"Pretty, I need to go get my shit from the crib. I left a lot of my stuff and I really don't want to have to start all over from scratch," informed KeeKee.

"I feel you," he responded. "So what you want to do?" he asked her, being supportive.

"I just want to go pack up a few suitcases. Baby, I know I'm going to have to leave certain things, but I want to at least get some of my shit. I'll go get it myself. I'll just take my car. You know I ain't going to pull no U-Haul truck up in the driveway or nothing like that. But I'm going to get some of my shit," she announced as PrettyBoy smiled, but it quickly faded.

"I don't know, baby, didn't' you say that he was getting out of the hospital yesterday or today or something like that? Plus that nigga might be there and start trippin' about you leaving," alerted PrettyBoy, as he was highly concerned.

"Baby, that nigga still asleep. I got his ugly ass, don't you worry about a thing. I'm going to be alright." She jumped from the bed buck naked and walked over to the bag she brought, pulling out a pair of jeans.

PrettyBoy watched as she got dressed and took a pull from the blunt, slowly inhaling the purp. KeeKee finished dressing and walked into the bathroom, shaking what her mama gave her.

"Say, KeeKee, baby?" PrettyBoy hollered towards the bathroom.

"What's up, daddy?" she yelled back.

He reached into the nightstand drawer and pulled out a .38 snub nose revolver just as KeeKee walked out of the bathroom and over to the bed. "Here, baby, take this with you, just in case," he said, handing her the gun.

She took it, put it in her purse, then kissed him on his lips, quickly saying, "I'll be right back." Then she walked towards the bedroom door, stopped, and turned around. "I love you," purred KeeKee.

"I love you too," replied PrettyBoy.

She blew him a kiss and ambled out of the house, all smiles.

***

Back at the house on Cascade, Snake and his crew were still in the room working on the safe. Well, they weren't working. They were stretched out on the floor, exhausted, drenched in sweat. They had managed to knock down most of the wall and could see the large safe staring them right in the face.

"Damn, ain't this a bitch," Snake growled

"This muthafucka must be protected by viper or some shit!"

The other fellas just shook their heads and lay there breathing hard.

Snake turned to one of his flunkies and asked, "Say, ain't we got a crowbar in the car out there?"

"It should be one in the trunk," the biggest one replied.

"Well, go get the muthafucka!" Snake yelled at him like he should've known his assignment.

The big dude looked at him hard, then slowly got up off his ass and walked out of the room. Once he made it to the bottom of the stairs, he went in the kitchen and poured himself a glass of Kool-Aid. It had plenty of sugar and was cold with the ice in it. He turned it up, drinking like a madman, while Kool-Aid ran down the side of his jaw.

"Ahhhh," the big dude said while wiping his mouth. Then he poured another glass and made his way out the front door. He walked towards the car with the glass of Kool-Aid in his hand.

"Well, go get the muthafucka," he said, mimicking Snake. "I don't know who the fuck he thinks I is," he mumbled, talking to himself. "That nigga got me fucked up," Big Boy said while opening the truck of the black SS Impala '96 that they came to the house in. He got the crowbar, slammed the trunk shut, and walked back to the house.

As he walked inside and closed the door, a gray Range Rover was pulling up into the driveway. He didn't even notice.

***

Tec looked over at Mario as he was bringing the car to a stop behind the black SS. Mario's eyes looked like he had just seen a ghost. Tec killed the engine and the music inside the Rover truck stopped.

"Well, I guess we'll just kill two birds with one stone," Tec said while reaching under the seat for his Baretta.

"I can't believe this bitch fucking the nigga in my house! This bitch gots to be crazy! Man, I'm about to kill this hoe," Mario growled, getting out of the Range Rover. He couldn't move as fast as he wanted to because he still was hurting from the shooting. He reached up under the passenger seat and got the two Glock 9s that Tec had stopped and gotten from his crib for him. Mario put the guns in his pockets as Tec got out of the truck.

"If anybody makes any crazy moves, we gon' kill both they asses right on the spot," Mario advised as they walked around the truck.

Tec shook just his head as they both walked towards the door of the house. The two guns hung from Mario's pockets the whole time. He wore gray State Property shorts and a jacket with a white T-shirt and black Tim boots. Tec didn't bother to tuck his gun in. He walked with his shit in his hand, ready to whack the first muthafucka he saw.

Trai'Quan

Chapter 14
It's either fight or surrender

In the house, Big Boy handed Snake the crowbar.

"'Bout time, nigga. What your ass do, take a lunch break?" snapped Snake, grabbing the crowbar.

Big Boy just stood there sippin' his Kool-Aid, thinking to himself, *This nigga trippin'!* Snake was just about to put the crowbar between the middle of the safe when he heard the front door of the house open.

Everybody in the room froze just as Big Boy dropped his glass of Kool-Aid.

***

When Mario walked through the door, he knew that he had figured shit out wrong. The whole living room had been ransacked. Muthafuckas was tryin' to rob him again. He heard a noise come from upstairs. He looked at the stairs and pulled out the two Glock-9s. Tec stepped inside the house right behind him, and closed the door. He looked at Mario in surprise as he took in the scene. Mario nodded his head towards the stairs as he lifted the two Glocks up in the sky, slowly moving in that direction. He put his back against the wall as he scaled the steps. Tec followed with his gun raised.

***

In the room upstairs, Snake had pulled out his Glock 40 handgun. The other three also went for their straps. Snake jumped from the closet and told the Big Dude and the guy closest to him, "You two stay in here." Then to the other one cat, he said, "You go in that room." He pointed to a room across the hall. "Whoever comes up here, we going to give them a little surprise," he finished before he ran from the room and got ready for the ambush.

***

KeeKee was in her white Lexus, coming from Decatur. *Damn*, she thought to herself, *this bitch does ride smooth*. Luckily, she had gotten Mario to put the car in her name. Shit, it wasn't every day a bitch got to own a Lexus with white interior with 20-inch rims and a system that didn't want it! Oh, she knew that she was beating down the block. Right now she had her system turned up, blasting Beyonce's new song…well, Destiny Child's new song, but we all know that means Beyonce. The song was titled "Cater to You".

"I'll cater to you, do anything for my man, I'll put my life in your hands…" she sang along as she rode. KeeKee knew that she wanted to spoil PrettyBoy. She thought about him as she passed through the west end area of Atlanta, headed towards Cascade. PrettyBoy was the type of nigga that she knew she wanted to spend the rest of her life with. So what if she had to set this ugly-ass nigga Mario up? He didn't love her. He didn't even know what love was. Well, he had gotten what was coming to him. Now she just wanted to get her shit and go!

***

Mario walked slowly up the stairs with his guns, leading the way with Tec right behind him. Mario couldn't help but to think about the possibility that it could be a nigga up here hurting KeeKee. The nigga probably had gotten all the bread out the safe and had beaten the bitch unconscious. *The safe!* An alarm went off in his head. *That's where them muthafuckas at*, he thought to himself. *Hell, the bitch was probably helping the nigga clean out the safe.*

He knew that it was crazy for him to still be thinking about her safety when she had almost had him killed. The doc had said that he was lucky to be alive. He was shot at point blank range: two to the stomach, one in the shoulder, and one in the chest. Shit, he was still in pain now and here he was thinking about this bitch that he was going to kill himself anyway. Hell, the bitch was already dead and he was going to make sure of that.

He made his way to the top of the stairs. All the doors were closed except the master bedroom. Mario could see from where he was standing that the room was a mess. He heard a noise coming from another room to his left, so he kicked the door in and fell back against the wall on the top of the staircase. The door flew in, and as soon as it did, shots were fired from inside the room.

Boom! Boom! Boom!

Mario stuck one of his guns through the threshold and returned fire.

Boom! Boom! Boom! Boom!

"Oh shittttt!" he heard someone yell.

Mario eased off the stairs and into the room. He saw a nigga on the ground bleeding.

"Oh shit, man, please don't kill me," the man begged with blood coming from his mouth. He was shot in the chest.

Tec walked up from the stairs with his gun still raised. As soon as he tried to peek into the room where Mario was, the door to the room where the safe was came flying open. Tec didn't even have time to get a shot off before a big-ass muthafucka rushed him like a football player. By the time he did manage to get a shot off, he was crashing through the hallway bathroom door. Just as that happened, all hell broke loose.

Mario heard the noise from the big gorilla rushing Tec and came out of the room pronto, but just then, another dude came out right behind the big dude bussing shots right at Mario. Shots were whizzing right by his head. He dove in the open room, landing on his back, and started releasing shots from his two Glocks. The guy came right around the corner shooting back at him.

Bullets from Mario's guns erupted into the man's chest, knocking blood and chunks of meat and flesh everywhere.

"Ohh! Ohh!" yelled the victim as his bullet-riddled body fell to the ground, depleted.

Mario lay flat on his back in excruciating pain from making the unexpected jump. Damn, he knew that was a close one. He looked back over his shoulder and noticed that the dude that he had shot earlier was still laying there, but now he had a gun in his hand and he was tryin' desperately to aim it at him. If he wouldn't have looked back, he would have had a hole in his head within a matter of seconds. Mario threw both of his arms back over his head and let his pistols rip. He tried not to think of the pain he was feeling in his body.

Boom! Boom! Boom!

"Uhhh…uhhh," the man moaned as he took his last breath of life.

***

In the bathroom, Tec was wrestling with the gorilla for his life. He had Tec's arms in a bear hug and had him pushed up against the sink. Tec used his feet and tried to push off the wall. The big dude put one of his hands around Tec's wrist that held the gun, and he put his other hand on Tec's throat and started to choke him.

"I'm going to kill you, muthafucka," the big man growled, spitting in Tec's face. \

Tec could feel himself getting weak. He knew that he couldn't give up this easy, so he used all the strength that he had left and pushed off the wall as hard as he could with his feet. He and the gorilla went flying through the glass shower door, landing in the tub. He landed on top of the gorilla, so he got to his feet fast. The big dude wasn't as lucky because most of his body was in the tub. He was still tryin' to grab ahold of something so he could get to his feet when Tec stood over him and emptied the clip of his Baretta in the monkey's face and body.

Just as Tec was about to walk out of the bathroom, Snake rushed out of the master bedroom and put the barrel of his gun to Mario's head. Mario was caught off guard, tryin' to get up from the floor. He was still hurting. He felt like he wouldn't be able to walk. He could feel pain all over his body. Snake didn't see Tec coming out of the bathroom. From the look of the scene, it looked like Mario had done all of the shooting. Snake waited until the shooting stopped before running out of the room.

Shit, now I'm finna murk everything moving, Snake thought implementing a survival tactic.

"You look like you havin' a hard time," mumbled Mario as he looked up.

Snake smiled and began to say, "Now drop them gu——"

He never had a chance to finish that sentence, because Tec had his gun to Snake's head, pushed up to his temple. "Drop the muthafuckin' gun, nigga! Now! Drop it, nigga!" Snake dropped the gun. When he did, Tec pulled the trigger.

Click!

Snake turned his body to make a move, but Tec was quicker. He tackled Snake, and they both went rolling down the stairs, fighting for their lives. It took everything Mario had to get to his feet, but he did, and he grabbed his two guns, rushing down the stairs.

Tec and Snake had made it all the way down the stairs and were now going blow for blow. Snake caught him with a good right hook and sent him to the floor hard, just as Mario was coming down the stairs.

Snake ran for the front door.

Trai'Quan

Chapter 15
It's a shitty affair!

When KeeKee pulled up to the house, her instinct told her to turn around and just ride off and don't look back, but she didn't listen. Plus she was thinking, *Well, I'm already in the driveway. It's too late now, I might as well go on in. Mario may have saw my car and if I pull off, I'll never be able to get my shit.* But her insides told her that something was up. Maybe it was the cars in the driveway. She knew that the Rover belonged to Tec, but whose Impala was that?

Well, it's probably some niggas Mario got to handle the bizness about him getting shot. He probably had to take the shit out on somebody, KeeKee thought as she got out of her car. She also thought that it was a shame that some innocent person was going to get hurt or probably killed for what she had done. *Oh well,* KeeKee thought. *It's all a part of the game, baby.*

As she passed the SS Impala, slowly making her way to the door of the house, she thought about how she would break up with Mario so she could go on living her life with PrettyBoy. Just as she made it to the door of the house, it swung open and Snake came running out but. Before he could make a full step out of the house, Mario's two Glock 9s drove shots through his body.

Boom! Boom! Boom!

Snake collapsed right on KeeKee, causing her to fall to the ground. She screamed at the top of her lungs while she lay under Snake's dead body, his blood dripping all over her.

"Oh my God! Ohhhhh!" she yelled.

***

Mario ran out of the house once he saw what had happened. His first instinct was to help KeeKee up, but he caught himself and looked back to see where Tec was. He was coming out of the house, holding his jaw.

"Hurry up, Tec, drag this nigga back inside the house!" Mario yelled over KeeKee's screams. "I got KeeKee!"

Tec grabbed Snake's dead boy and dragged him inside. KeeKee got to her feet, shaking and crying with her hand over her mouth while Mario held her arm and walked her into the house. As soon as the front door closed, she screamed "Oh my God, what happened, Mario!"

He just looked at her while she stared at the wreckage the burglars had made of the place. Then she noticed Mario staring at her.

"Bitch!" he yelled as he backhand slapped her to the floor. "Bitch, you know what the fuck happened, bitch! You set me up! That's what happened, bitch!" he yelled as he kicked her in her stomach.

"Ooohhhh," she groaned as she balled up in the fetal position.

He grabbed her by her ponytail. "Get up, bitch!"

KeeKee then tried to plead for her life. "Baby, I don't...I don't know what's going on. I didn't have nothing to do with this."

Mario got even madder. "Don't give me that baby shit, bitch!" he spat back at her, slapping her with the pistol, knocking her out cold.

"Call some of the fellas and tell them to get over here fast. We got to get rid of these bodies," he said to Tec.

Tec walked over to the phone.

"We gon' burn this muthafucka house to the ground, my nigga." He looked around the room, which now has painted red with blood. Tec looked at him, then somebody on the other line answered the phone. "What's up, man? Aye look, I need some of y'all niggas to get over here to Mario's spot ASAP," informed Tec.

While he talked on the phone, Mario was pacing the room, walking back and forward. "Damn, what's that gotdamn smell?" Mario asked Tec. "It smells like shit in this bitch," he said, fanning the air with his hands.

"Huh?" asked Tec, taking his attention from the conversation he was having on the phone.

Mario looked down at himself and notice that the shit bag he had on must have busted because shit now stained his white T-shirt. "Damn" He said, looking diseased. "Man, I got to go change." He started heading up the staircase.

"Oh yeah, bring some gas too. We gon' have to torch the place," Tec said into the phone and disconnected.

Chapter 16
Sexy Redd

PrettyBoy walked out of the townhome in Decatur. He had changed into a green Sean John leather jacket with all-black fitty cap. He walked up to the Malibu he had just bought and had painted money green with black racing stripes. The black tinted windows and the black interior made the car look real mean. The chrome 24-inch rims didn't help matters much nor did the chrome pipes he had hanging out the back end of the car. He had himself a monster. PrettyBoy jumped in the car and he pulled out of the parking space, on the way to take the car for a spin around the block. He crunk his sound system up as loud as it could go.

"Un, un, un… I can't deny it, I'm a straight rider, you don't want to fuck with me…" 2 Pac blasted from the speakers.

PrettyBoy could feel the bass coming from the four 12-inch speakers he had in the trunk as he bobbed his head to the music. He drove through the apartment complex, punching the gas pedal to the floor, showing off how fast his car could run. He made his way from the front of the apartment complex, headed towards the back.

The front of Lantana apartments were nice-looking townhouses, but the back apartments were cramped together, one on top of the other. They had hallways that had become the hustling spots. The junkies, thugs, and the girls in the hood all hung in the back of the complex along with every other form of street life. Today was no exception. PrettyBoy could see that everybody was out in full effect as he swerved through the neighborhood. He saw a group of females standing in front of one of the buildings, outside kicking it. He swerved right in front of them and brought the car to a quick stop. He just sat there and looked at them through the window.

He saw a thick redbone in the midst of the crowd. She wore her hair in braids; it was brown. She had on a pair of Gucci shades, but he could still tell who she was. He knew that frame from anywhere: 36-23-36. She had on a sky-blue Baby Phat top and some jeans that looked like they were painted on her. The girls strained their eyes tryin' to look inside the car's dark tinted windows.

"Girl, who the fuck that is?" one of the broads asked.

"Shit, girl, I don't know," one of the other girls shot back.

PrettyBoy sat inside the car rolling a blunt while the girl talked outside the window. After he finished, he fired the blunt up and let the passenger window roll down from a button he pushed on the driver's side door panel.

"Say Red!" PrettyBoy yelled through the window while cutting the music down.

Red looked inside the car, still not knowing who he was. She slowly walked to the car, and finally, she got close enough to see that it was PrettyBoy. "Oh shit, what's up, baby?" Red said as she ran to the car and leaned into the window. "Shit, I didn't know who the fuck you was, boy."

"What's up?" asked PrettyBoy, tapping the gas lightly, exhaling.

Red turned around and yelled back to her girlfriends, "Y'all, it's PrettyBoy, y'all!"

"Oh, okay," they all said in response with smiles on their faces.

"So what's up, Red, what you been getting into lately?" PrettyBoy said as she turned back to face him.

"Well, you know me, a little bit of this, and a little bit of that," Red said, real sexy-like.

"Well, you know what they say, shawty, if it don't make dollars, it don't make sense." he told her with his hands in the air.

"Sho' you right. I see you got yourself another car," she complimented, admiring the car.

"Yeah," he replied, faking a pull from the blunt. "Check this out, Red. I'm putting together some real shit. I could use a real bitch like you on my team. I think we can get a lot of money together."

She looked him in the eyes and said, "I'm feeling that."

So he went on. "Look, here go my number, baby girl," he said as he grabbed pen and paper and started to write. "Just hit me up on my cell. We gon' talk," he finished, handing her the number.

"Alright, that's what's up," she said as she took the number, and then paused for a second. "But you ain't tryin' to have me selling pussy for you and shit, is you?"

"Nall, baby." PrettyBoy laughed. "This on some bigger and better shit. I want you to be a part of my family."

"Yeah, this some of that pimp shit, but I'm going to call you anyway, boy," Red admitted as they both began to laugh.

"Alright, shawty, be easy," he stated as he departed.

"Yeah, PrettyBoy, keep it pimpin'," she shot back, smiling at him as she backed away from the car.

He turned the music up and pulled off with the tires screaming. That was his way of letting the hood know that his Malibu was souped up. Some niggas from the hood saw him pass and threw up the deuces. By this time, everyone in the hood knew that it was PrettyBoy in the car. He hit the horn twice and kept pushing.

Trai'Quan

Chapter 17
It's now or never

When KeeKee woke up, the whole side of her face hurt, and she was in the back seat of her car, sitting next to Mario. He had changed into an Atlanta Falcons Deon Sanders throwback jersey, black jeans, and a pair of custom made Air Force Ones. KeeKee laid with her head leaned against the door. She felt like she had been hit with a ton of bricks. She knew that her head was swollen, and her face too. At first she couldn't remember shit, then it all came back to her. *Oh shit*, she thought as she pondered on a way to get out of this. *Run! Run, run, run, run, now!*

Mario saw her body language and read it. "Bitch, unless you want another knot on your head, or a hole in that muthafucka, you better not do shit stupid," he warned while watching her closely.

She looked away from him, knowing that he had read her thoughts, then she noticed that they were still at the house, parked in the driveway. There were more people walking in and out of the house, plus a white van was pulled up to the front door.

Oh my God, KeeKee thought to herself in horror as she watched a group of men load what she knew were three dead bodies covered in black trash bags into the van.

Tec walked over to the car and got in the passenger seat. He saw that KeeKee purse was in the seat, so he grabbed it and threw it in the back, hitting her in the face.

"Bitch, get this shit out this muthafuckin' seat, you maggot-ass bitch." he yelled as he sat down while KeeKee screamed when the purse hit her.

"So what's up now, Mario?" Tec asked, looking back at Mario.

"You told Tray to come and drive us to the spot?" Mario asked, making sure everything was everything.

"Yeah! Here he comes now," Tec answered, watching him approach through the windshield.

Tray was a little slim, dark-skinned dude who worked for Mario. He got into the car and started the engine. He didn't ask any questions as he pulled the car out of the driveway. As they rode, nobody talked.

They just rode in silence. While they rode, KeeKee thought about Pret-tyBoy, about how they wouldn't have a chance to ever make love again, because she knew she was dead. They were definitely going to kill her. She couldn't believe that her life would end like this. She dropped her head and started to think about her life.

God, please, if you could just get me out of this... God, I promise you, I'll change, God, I'll do anything, please, God, please don't let them hurt me anymore. She started to pray to herself as tears slowly formed in her eyes. Then she noticed her purse was laying in her lap. She looked at it as she thought about the gun PrettyBoy had given her to take with her earlier that day. She couldn't believe her luck. The dumb-ass nigga Tec had thrown it right to her. Now she would have a chance to kill all these bitch-ass niggas. She would kill Mario first, for everything he had done to her, even though she never had shot a gun before, in her life.

The car turned on Ashby Road and was headed towards MLK Dr.

"Say shawty, you put everything in the trunk?" Mario asked Tec, double-checking the mission at hand.

"Yeah, folk," he responded quickly.

"Bet. When we get to the spot, I want you to go back and get them niggas' car out my driveway. We got to get rid of that too before we start the fire."

"Check. I got you, my nigga," Tec assured as the car was turning on Hamilton E Homes Road.

KeeKee knew that it was either now or never. She was probably in for some real pain. Fuck that, she had other plans. She slowly unzipped, her purse tryin' not to look down. Zzzzzzzzz...

Mario looked her way, and she stopped and tensed up. He stared at her, and she turned her head and looked out of the window. The whole time her heart was beating a mile a minute. Finally, Mario turned his gaze towards his window. KeeKee finished unzipping the purse. She got it open. She started to put her hand inside the purse, then Mario turned and caught her.

"What the fuck?" he yelled as he dove to grab her purse.

She came up with the revolver in her hand. He grabbed her wrist just as she licked off a shot.

The bullet hit the driver right in the back of the head. That's when all hell broke loose.

The driver slumped over and the car went wild while Mario and KeeKee struggled for the gun in the back seat. KeeKee licked another shot right into the ceiling of the car.

While this was going on in the back seat, Tec was up front struggling to gain control of the car. They had just missed a head on collision because he had grabbed the steering wheel. He swerved the car over into a side street and stomped the brakes. Mario yanked the gun from KeeKee's grip and went to choking her, while she kicked and screamed.

"Bitch, I should kill you right here, bitch!" He put the gun to her head and yelled, "Stop movin', bitch, stop movin'!" But she was hysterical. "Fuck it!" he said, then he hit her with the pistol, causing her to black out again. All KeeKee saw was darkness...

Trai'Quan

Chapter 18
We ready

PrettyBoy was on I-20 going west. The Malibu was flying through traffic. He knew something was up when he kept trying to call KeeKee and he didn't get no answer. He had just threw the cell phone down and was on his way to meet up with Jarvis and Mac so they could ride over there to the nigga Mario's house, and see what was up. He swerved the Malibu from lane to lane. He drove like a race car driver, like someone's life depended on him, and at that time, he really did believe someone's life did, and that someone was KeeKee. He picked the cell phone back up from the passenger seat and called to the spot in Cobb County to see if Jarvis and Mac had made it there yet.

"Yeah" Jarvis answered on the second ring.

"Yeah, man, I was just checking to see if y'all had made it there," PrettyBoy said, almost running into the back of a red Toyota. He swerved the Malibu over and shot past the car.

"Yeah, we just got here, folk. We waiting on you, everything ready, we got everything straight," Jarvis said on the other end.

"Bet, my nigga. I'm on 20, I'm about to get off at Six Flags, I'll be there in about five minutes or less," informed PrettyBoy with his feet on the gas.

"Alright, folk."

Once PrettyBoy made it off the interstate, he drove hard down Six Flags Drive until he made it to Crestview townhomes, the neighborhood that they were meeting at. He rode down a hill until he came to a blue townhome. The driveway was filled with cars, all older models: Chevys, Pontiacs, Buicks. He killed the engine and jumped out of the car, but before he made it to the door, it opened and Mac stood in the threshold.

"Everything's in the living room," he told PrettyBoy as he walked into the house.

Once he got inside, PrettyBoy could see that there were about six people in the living room and kitchen area. Mike sat on the sofa with his arm still in a sling. In front of him lay an AK-47 with two clips taped together, a bulletproof vest, and three Mac-11 machine guns.

There were three younger members of the crew in the kitchen, sitting at the table cutting up crack cocaine and putting it in little baggies.

"I thought I told you to sit your ass down and chill," PrettyBoy said to Mike.

"Shiiitt, my nigga, this is chilling for me," Mike replied, using his good hand to gesture what was going on around the house.

PrettyBoy took off his money green leather jacket and revealed the Desert Eagles he had in his shoulder holsters. Then he took off the coasters and his shirt next. After that, he picked up the bulletproof vest and put it on. While he was getting dressed again, Jarvis asked, "What car you want to take?"

"We'll take mine," PrettyBoy answered, then he said to Mike, "I want you to keep chillin'. I might just be overreacting. It might not be that serious my nigga."

"That's cool, shawty. I'm going to just chill here, but y'all niggas call if some shit jump off," Mike quickly shot back

"That's a bet," PrettyBoy assured as he was walking towards the door.

Mac snatched up a Mac-11 from the table and said, "Let's ride," as he followed him and Jarvis out of the house.

When they got to the car, Mac got in the back seat, and Jarvis took the front. PrettyBoy jumped in the driver's seat and took off.

Chapter 19
In Center Hill

On Hamilton E Holmes Road, Tec hopped out of the passenger seat of KeeKee's Lexus. They were still parked on the side street where he had pulled the car over at. He walked over to the driver's side door and opened it.

"Damn!" he yelled, looking at Tray's body slumped back in the seat. "Ain't this a bitch? This bitch done killed Tray!" he repeated over and over with disgust in his voice. "Damn!" he yelled again while staring at his homeboy's body.

Tec then grabbed Tray's arm and pulled him out of the car. His body fell hard to the concrete. Tec jumped in the car and pulled off. They made a couple of turns, and then they were on Bankhead Highway. Then they turned off Bankhead and were on Center Hill, where they pulled into the driveway of an old brown house that looked as if it was halfway submerged. They both got out of the car and quickly carried KeeKee in the house. Tec carried her legs, and Mario had her upper body. Once they were inside the little house, they took her down into the basement, Mario was tired so he said "fuck it" and dropped her. Her head struck the hard concrete. Tec looked away, thinking, *Damn*, then he dropped her feet.

"Look, I'm going to handle this. You go take care of that bizness with the house. Get that car and just leave shawty shit somewhere and we'll go back and get her shit later. And make sure you break a back window or something before you set the crib on fire so we can make it look like a break-in," Mario said.

"You think them folks going to go for that shit?" Tec asked, thinking, *That sounds kinda corny!*

"Hell yeah, but you got to make sure you do that shit, because you know how them detectives and insurance folks like to investigate and shit," Mario shot back with a half a laugh.

"Hell, they be tryin' to solve the muthafuckin' case, homes," Tec agreed with a grimace.

"So handle your bizness, man. Let me got get my bread out this trunk before you skate," Mario told him, easing up the steps.

"Alright, bet," he said as he watched him head up the stairs.

After Mario disappeared, he stared at KeeKee as she lay stretched out on the floor with her legs wide open.

"Bitch, I should take some of that pussy before it get cold," he joked, then licked his lips. "Nall, bitch, you got that killer pussy," he quickly amended, shaking his head, erasing the thought from his mind.

A few minutes later, Tec heard Mario making his way back down the stairs. He came into view with two large army duffle bags in both of his hands.

"Whew!" he mumbled, dropping the heavy bags

"I'll be right back, my nigga," Tec replied while leaving the room. He was eager to go implement the orders that Mario had given him.

Chapter 20
It's time to handle business

PrettyBoy was thinking hard while listening to the music in the Malibu. DMX was sayin' in his song, "I gotta live my life, like it's one more move to make, one more road to cross, one more rule to break..." Heavy blunt smoke was circulating in the car. PrettyBoy leaned over and cut the music down some.

"Ah, I got a bad feeling, my nigga. This shit is far from over, I believe a lot more muthafuckas gon' have to die about this shit," he said to everybody in the car.

"So be it," Mac replied, shaking his head up and down like he was ready for war.

"As long as it ain't muthafuckin' us!" Jarvis said while handing Mac the blunt.

"Believe it," Mac agreed.

"Yeah, fo' sho'," shot PrettyBoy as he turned the music back up and smashed the gas, sending that thing sideways up the street.

***

Tec got back to the house on Cascade in no time. He rode right past the house.

"Damn, where I'm going to park this muthafucka?" he asked to himself.

Then he saw a white church coming up the street to his left. He slung the car into the parking lot. Tec got out of the car and started to walk off, not even bothering to lock the doors. He ambled down the street towards the house.

When he got to the house, he eased up the driveway and saw that the SS Impala was the only car there. He had told his homebody to take his Range Rover with them when they left, and he was glad to see that they did. He already had his hands full for today. He just hoped that they had left the gasoline in the house like Mario had told them to. He made his way to the back door, not even noticing the black Mustang that was parked across the street.

In the black Mustang were two of GridLock's goons. They had already been inside the house once they saw Snake's car outside. After they saw that the house was wrecked and blood was all over the floor, they had called GridLock instantly. GridLock had given them strict orders to keep an eye on the place and call as soon as they saw some activity, and that's exactly what they had done.

"Yo, GridLock!" Marks said into his Nextel cell phone two-way radio.

"Yo!" GridLock's voice came back through the receiver.

"I just saw one kid walk up to the house," Mark informed. "You want us to go in and jump him?"

" Nall, kid, wait and see what he does and then when he comes out, follow him…then jump him," GridLock replied.

"10-4," Mark said back into the phone then he turned to look at Rico.

Mark and Rico were both New Yorkers from Brooklyn. Mark was a brown-skinned chubby cat. Rico looked Puerto Rican. He had on army fatigue gloves with a white T-shirt and an army fatigue hat, with black army pants and Timberland Boots Mark wore an army fatigue jacket with all black on.

"Yo, you heard the man, I guess we got to just wait," Mark said to Rico.

"Yo, what the fuck is this cat doing in there?" Rico asked while looking towards the house.

"I don't know, kid. It's some real fucked up shit going down, son!" Mark assured while staring at the crib.

"Yo, if this muthafucka don't come out in a minute, son, I'm going in there," Rico said in his heavy New York accent as they sat back and waited.

***

A couple of minutes later, Tec was coming out of the front door of the house. He was moving fast. He walked over to the black SS Impala, jumped in the driver's seat, and took off. Mark slowly pulled out from across the street and began to follow him. He followed the car as it sped down the two-lane road.

Tec drove to the nearest gas station. He wanted to run inside to grab some blunts and a little something to snack on. He pulled up to the side of the building. It was a small brick store. Tec was getting out of the car when the Mustang shot up beside him. Rico hung out of the window with a .357 revolver pointed straight at Tec.

"You feel lucky, kid, huh, you feel lucky?" Rico yelled with the murder weapon in his face.

Tec threw his hands up in the air. Mark was jumping out the driver's side by then and Rico started to get out. Before Tec had a chance to do anything, Mark had walked up with a .45 pointed at him, and he didn't break a step in his stride before smacking Tec right in the head with the pistol. Tec went down hard and Mark grabbed him by the shirt and yelled, "Get up, muthafucka."

Tec stood to his feet with the help of Mark while Rico stood back with his gun pointed at him.

"Pop the trunk!" Mark told Rico as he took the pistol from under Tec's shirt. Then he walked him over to the trunk of the Mustang and through him inside.

"Let's ride, baby." Mark smiled and belligerently slammed the trunk.

The two then got inside the car and pulled off fast, completely lost in the night.

Trai'Quan

Chapter 21
Shit done got dumb real!

PrettyBoy and his partners were riding down Cascade when Jarvis spotted KeeKee's Lexus parked in the church parking lot.

"Aye, ain't that KeeKee shit right there?" he asked PrettyBoy as they were passing the street.

PrettyBoy looked and when he saw the car, he slung the Malibu around and sped into the parking lot. Once the car stopped, they all jumped out. PrettyBoy went to the driver's seat and everybody circled around the car. No KeeKee, but they all noticed the bullet hole in the top of the ceiling and all the blood that was on the front seat. Water came to PrettyBoy's eyes as he stared at the driver's seat. They all stood there and stared at the car.

"Damn!" PrettyBoy finally broke the silence. "Damn!" he repeated, slamming the car door shut. "Man, let's go kill this pussy-ass nigga," he said with a look in his eyes that had to mean death. Then he stormed toward the Malibu and the fellas ran to the car.

"Let's do this," Mac growled before getting into the car.

Once PrettyBoy's Malibu pulled out into the street, he saw the fire trucks shoot past him and heard all types of sirens. All of the fellas looked at each other and as the car pulled into traffic close enough to see Mario's house, they saw why. The whole house was on fire. Fire trucks along with police cars were all over the yard and driveway. People were outside watching and police were walking around talking to the neighbors.

PrettyBoy was in deep thought as he sat in traffic, trying to decipher the issue and dilemma at hand.

***

"Get the fuck out the car!" Rico yelled, looking in the trunk with his .357 pointed at Tec.

Tec slowly climbed out of the trunk, realizing that he was in somebody's backyard. He heard a dog barking as he looked around and saw a mean-ass pitbull tryin' to break the chain to get loose. Mark stood there watching as he got out of the trunk. Once Tec got out, he noticed that the door to the house was open, a door leading directly to the basement.

"In there." Mark pointed with the gun.

Tec started to walk in, he walked through the threshold and he didn't like what he saw: some big muthafucka with a cigar in his mouth, dressed in all black fatigues with a skull cap on. In his hand was a hammer that he kept hitting in the palm of his hand, up and down. The big dude said, "It's hammer time, baby."

Tec tried to make a break back out the door, but Mark clapped him with a hard hit to the head with his gun. Lights out…

Chapter 22
Firepower

When KeeKee woke up this time, she was in a chair and Mario was on his knees tying her legs to the chair. He had already tied her hands behind her back. Mario looked up when he saw her gaining consciousness.

"Where am I?" she moaned, still not all the way awake.

"You on death row, bitch, and your ass in the chair!" Mario shot back at her, then he finished tying the rope around her legs.

As he stood up, she began to talk. "Ooohh, Mario, listen," she begged.

"What? What the fuck you got to say?" Mario yelled, really sick and tired of hearing her voice.

"Baby, I'm sorry, please don't kill me," KeeKee begged for her life.

"Bitch, you already dead. I tell you what. You tell me who the niggas was and I'll make it fast," Mario assured her.

KeeKee deliberated on it for a second. "You killed him. That was him at the house. I don't know——"

Mario had hit her with a hard right before she could get the rest of her words out, causing blood to spill out of KeeKee's mouth. "Hoe, I know GridLock sent them niggas to the crib to get at me. I saw the NY plates. I think that's them niggas who robbed us!" Mario informed while he reached over and picked up the duct tape from a nearby table. "I don't want to hear shit else. I got other ways to make you talk." Mario smirked as he duct taped KeeKee's mouth shut.

***

PrettyBoy and his crew were riding down Hollywood Road. He had decided, what better time than now to get more guns? They were going to meet up with Jarvis and Mac's uncle about the guns he wanted to get.

Big Nard was known on Hollywood Road. He was what they called a real OG. He had been terrorizing the streets of the westside of Atlanta for a while now - shootouts, robberies, and murders. He was a monster, and Mac and Jarvis were proud to have him as an uncle.

The Malibu turned into the Hollywood west projects. The brick buildings that looked like they didn't own any form of life stared back at them through the car's window. Nobody was outside. Well, it seemed that way until PrettyBoy pulled the car into a dead end, at the back of the neighborhood. The neighborhood was a one way in, one way out. To outsiders, it may have felt like a death trap, but to the boys, it was just like home. A few men stood by their doors in groups once PrettyBoy made it to the dead end. He stopped the car and they all piled out.

"What's up with y'all young niggas?" Big Nard called from one of the groups in the corner. He was standing in between some guys looking like big fat don. He was a big black dude, about 300 pounds. He wore a black derby hat, a navy blue silk shirt, and navy-blue slacks with black shoes. Once the fellas were walking up on him, he threw his arms open, saying, "What's up, baby, how y'all livin'?" He had a big cigar in his hand.

"Unc, we need to talk," Mac said.

"Cool, cool, y'all chill," Big Nard said once he saw that the boys looked pissed off, like something was definitely wrong.

"Say, y'all fellas excuse us for a minute. I need to holla at my nephews, baby," he stated to the dudes he was standing with.

As they walked off, Jarvis spoke. "You remember we said we wanted to get more of them vests and them guns, right?"

"Not to worry, baby boy, I got that covered,"' Big Nard told him. "What's on your mind, PrettyBoy? You just standing there looking like a ghost."

"Nall, Unc, it's this beef with this nigga, man. I'm ready to get this shit over with," PrettyBoy admitted.

"Alright, baby, I got something just for that. Come on," Big Nard announced, walking out into the street as the boys followed. He walked over to a dark gray '04 Jaguar, and a dude was sitting on the trunk. He motioned for the dude to get up as he came towards the car. Big Nard pulled a key from his pocket and placed it inside the key hole in the trunk, and it popped open. The boys all stood around, looking in. "Now that's what I call heavy artillery," Big Nard said with a smile on his face the size of Cali.

The trunk was filled with AR-15s, M16s, AK-47s, revolvers, handguns, pumps, and a few bulletproof vests and extra clips. The boys' eyes lit up like the 4th of July.

"That's what I'm muthafuckin' talking about," Jarvis said in elation.

PrettyBoy quickly asked, "How much you want for the whole trunk?" He could already taste revenge.

Trai'Quan

Chapter 23
I want answers

When Tec came to, all he could see was stars. He shook his head and tried to clear his mind so he could think.

Smack! "Wake up!" Smack! "Wake up!" GridLock was slapping the hell out of him.

"Oh shit!" Tec yelled from the pain of the blows.

"Yeah, that's it. You can't miss the party," GridLock said to Tec, bending down, looking him in the eyes.

Tec was tied to a chair in the dark basement with his hands behind his back and his legs to the chair, all secured with duct tape. He looked up and saw Mark and Rico standing behind the cat that was in his face and he knew he wasn't going to make it out of there alive

"Okay, I see that you're with us," GridLock said standing straight up.

"Uhhh," Tec moaned. "What the fuck going on, man?"

"You want to know what's going on? I'll tell you what the fuck is going on?" GridLock said, pacing back and forth in front of Tec. "I lost my man Mouse over some bullshit, not to mention the twenty birds that I got hit for. And you know what? I believe your man Mario knows more than he claims to know. Now you got caught in Snake's car, so you know where Mario at."

"Man," Tec broke in and said, "Mario ain't have shit to do with that."

GridLock stopped and stared at him. "How the fuck do you know?" he asked.

"I'm telling you, man, the bitch had him set up," Tec shot back with no hesitation.

"What bitch?" asked GridLock quizzically.

"His bitch, man, the one that was at the club that night," Tec answered the question.

GridLock just looked at him for a while, letting it all soak in. "Yo, y'all killed Snake and them?" he asked.

"Shit, we didn't have a choice," replied Tec.

GridLock stared at him with a grimace.

"So you going to make this easy, or do you want to make this shit hard?" GridLock asked. "Where's Mario?"

Tec didn't say shit. He just looked at the dude with the big cigar in his mouth and stared him in the eyes.

"Yep, you like it ruff," GridLock assumed with an evil smile on his face. Then he turned to Mark and said, "Give me the hammer." Mark handed him the hammer he had been holding. "Take his shoes off, then get behind him and keep him still," GridLock ordered.

Rico put the .357 he had been holding in the small of his back, took Tec's shoes and socks off, and went behind him and held him down.

"Look, man, you got to believe me, a nigga ain't bullshittin'. It was the bitch," Tec said.

GridLock smiled and said, "I always wanted to do this shit, ever since I saw it in that movie." GridLock walked up to him with the hammer in his hand.

"Nall, man, don't, you 'bout to hit my toes and shit," Tec pled, on the verge of tears.

"Nall, son, I'm 'bout to hit your whole muthafuckin' feet," Grid-Lock corrected, bringing the hammer down crashing on one of Tec's feet.

"Oooohhhh, oooohhh, shit!" Tec screamed as the excruciating pain overtook his body.

"Oh, we gon' get some answers!" GridLock said as he raised the hammer again, thinking to himself, *This MF gon' tell me what I wanna know, or else…*

Chapter 24
Somebody got to pay

After duct taping KeeKee's mouth, Mario went upstairs. KeeKee could hear him walking around in the house as she began to try to free herself. The ropes on her hands weren't that tight. She knew that she could get them loose if she kept at it, but would it be before Mario got back? It had to be! She worked the rope up and down ,moving her hands. Finally, it started to come a loose. She hurried up and freed her hands, then went to work on her feet. Once she was free, she jumped to her feet. She looked around the old dirty basement for a weapon. In a corner by a heater, she found an old, rusty, metal pipe. KeeKee grabbed the pipe and stormed towards the staircase. She walked up the flight of stairs like a person that was ready to either kill or die. When she opened the door and walked into the upper part of the house, she didn't see anyone there. She made a run for the door, but before she got there, she heard someone coming down the steps. She ran over to the old sofa in the living room and knelt behind it. She held the pipe in her hand and tried not to breathe too hard. Mario made his way into the living room.

"Yeah, alright bet," Mario said into the cell phone. "If you see that nigga, hit me up," he consulted before hanging up the phone. He walked over to a small table in front of the sofa, picked up a blunt, set the phone down, and went back up the stairs. Mario didn't even notice that the basement door was wide open.

KeeKee heard him making his way up the steps and jumped up. She saw the phone on the table. She ran over and picked it up before she ran out the front door of the house. She ran for the street with all she had, but once she was running down the street, she realized that she didn't know where she was. She saw the road that led to the highway, and she ran for it. Once she got on the street, she looked up with tears in her eyes, barely able to read the sign that said Bankhead Highway. KeeKee went to pressing buttons on the phone presto. PrettyBoy…she had to call PrettyBoy, he would come save her.

That's all she could think of as she walked down the highway with the phone ringing in her ear.

***

PrettyBoy and the crew were riding through a back street, just coming from Hollywood Road. They were in the car talking while listening to Young Jeezy's CD *Trap or Die*.

"Shawty, with the shit we got in the trunk, we could start a war," Jarvis bragged to Mac in the back seat. "Yeah, niggas gon' feel this shit," Jarvis went on.

"Yeah, Unc looked out then" Mac said from the back seat.

PrettyBoy's phone went off.

"Answer the phone, PrettyBoy." Jarvis said.

PrettyBoy was so caught up in KeeKee's death that he didn't even hear the phone ringing, and it was sitting right on his lap. The music in the car wasn't even up loud.

"Oh," said PrettyBoy as he picked the phone up from his lap. "Speak to me!" he said into the receiver.

"Hello? PrettyBoy!" KeeKee yelled into the phone.

"Hello?" PrettyBoy yelled back, flabbergasted, as KeeKee started to cry.

"Baby, I'm hurt, they beat me up."

"Where you at?" PrettyBoy yelled into the phone. "Baby, where you at?"

"I'm on Bankhead Highway. I'm walking. I just passed Church Street," KeeKee replied, still crying.

"Look, baby, I'm right down the street. You just keep walking and stay on the phone with me," PrettyBoy said, turning the Malibu down a street, punching the gas.

"What's up?" Jarvis yelled, syncing that something wasn't right.

"What it is?" Mac asked as well.

"It's KeeKee. She alive, man, she alive," PrettyBoy answered jubilantly.

He turned the Malibu on Bankhead, flying. He was only on the street for a couple of seconds before he saw KeeKee. As the car made its way towards her, his eyes filled with water. Her heart skipped a beat when she saw PrettyBoy's car push up on the curve. He almost jumped out of the car before it stopped. He ran to her and she met him half way. He grabbed her into his arms "Baby, you alright?" he asked quizzically.

"Yeah, I'm alright," KeeKee replied back through tears.

"I'm gon' get the niggas who did this to you. Come on, let's get inside the car," PrettyBoy informed as they walked to the car and quickly hopped in the back seat.

Trai'Quan

Chapter 25
War zone

Tec was going in and out of consciousness as blood was dripping from his feet. He knew he'd never walk again. His feet looked like two squashed mushrooms, two squished human mushrooms, dripping blood. His feet lay in a pool of his own blood.

"Ooohhh," Tec moaned from the excruciating pain.

"Now I'm going to quit torturing you," GridLock said, walking over to the old deep freezer they kept in the basement.

Tec looked around and didn't see anybody but GridLock with his back to him, getting something out of the deep freezer. Tec still couldn't forgive himself for telling where Mario was because he knew that they would kill Mario. The two goons were probably already on their way over there to do it now. Well, he knew that he wasn't going to make it out of here alive, so hell, they would die together.

GridLock came out of the freezer with a chainsaw. He looked at Tec and smiled with the cigar hanging out of the corner of his mouth. "I hope you don't get frostbite, muthafucka."

GridLock crunk up the chainsaw and walked over to Tec to take him out of his misery, limb by limb.

***

While PrettyBoy and KeeKee sat in the back seat, she told him everything that had happened. He held her in his arms tightly, caressing and comforting her.

"You say that they had you in a house?" PrettyBoy asked her, again, tryna pinpoint the spot and area.

"Yeah," KeeKee answered.

"Where was the house at?" PrettyBoy continued.

"It was on Center Hill. I read the sign," KeeKee replied, still having flashbacks.

"I know where that's at. I'm going to need you to show me where the house at, baby, alright?" PrettyBoy said eagerly, anxious to get revenge.

"Alright," KeeKee replied.

"Mac, turn on Center Hill Road," PrettyBoy said as the car moved along.

The Malibu turned on Center Hill Road and came to a stop in front of an old brown house.

"That's the one," KeeKee said with terror in her eyes.

Mac stopped the car across the street and parked.

"Baby, stay in the car. I'll be right back," PrettyBoy instructed as he got out of the car along with Mac and Jarvis right on his heels. The fellas all walked to the back of the car.

"Look, Jarvis, you stay out here with shawty. Mac, me and you going in," PrettyBoy said.

Jarvis shook his head in a manner to say yes while Mac opened the trunk. Mac handed PrettyBoy an AR-15 and he took an AK-47 from the trunk for himself.

"I'm going in through the front. You take the back," PrettyBoy told Mac. Then he said to Jarvis, "If somebody comes out the house, you kill 'em."

Then he and Mac approached the house. Mac went around the side of the house.

PrettyBoy walked up to the front door and shot the lock off. He kicked the door in, never stopping or breaking his stride. Once he walked inside, he saw Mario dive over the old sofa.

PrettyBoy lit up the sofa, tearing chunks out of it. Mario was behind the sofa, lying flat on his stomach with his hands covering his head.

Rat, tat, tat, tat!

Mario knew he had to make a play for it. He reached for his pistol at his waist. Once he got it out, he cradled the corner of the sofa and hung his Glock out from behind the couch and busted back.

Boom, boom, boom!

PrettyBoy jumped against the wall outside of the house. Mario got up from behind the sofa and made a run for the stairs.

Rat, tat, tat, tat!

PrettyBoy turned to fire just as Mario hit the stairs.

Rat, tat, tat, tat, click, click.

Shots went flying into the wall, just inches away from Mario, until he ran out of bullets.

As soon as PrettyBoy heard the gun click, he threw it down and made a run for Mario up the stairs. He knew that Mario had a gun, but it was like some mad and demented force was driving him.

When Mario saw him coming, he let off a few rounds behind him as he ran up the stairs. PrettyBoy jumped back and put his back against the wall.

"Oh, ain't no use in running, nigga!" PrettyBoy yelled as he pulled the two Desert Eagles from his shoulder holsters under his leather jacket. Then he dashed up the stairs behind Mario with his guns leading the way.

***

Outside, a black Mustang had just pulled up. Jarvis saw the car coming and put his hand under his shirt on his 9-millimeter handgun.

The Mustang pulled up fast and Mark tried to jump out of the driver's seat with his .45 already out the window, but as he attempted to get out of the car, Jarvis sat him back down with a hot slug from his 9mm. Mark hit the seat, then fell out of the car between the doors. Rico came from over the roof, licking shots from his 357. Jarvis returned fire, while KeeKee laid down in the backseat, screaming at the top of her lungs as her whole life flashed before her eyes, forcing her to pray.

"Oh God, please, not again…"

***

Mario was upstairs in a back bedroom, about to climb out the window, when PrettyBoy walked to the door of the room.

Boom, boom!

PrettyBoy sent multiple shots at him.

Boom, boom!

Mario answered back, assuring PrettyBoy that he wasn't going out without a fight. PrettyBoy went down. He was hit.

Mario tried to climb out of the window and was almost all the way out.

"Aye!" someone called out to him. "I want you to see it coming."

Mario looked and it was Mac standing in the backyard with an AK-47.

Boom, boom, boom, boom!

The slugs caught Mario all over his body, sending blood, guts, and bone marrow all types of ways as he fell to the ground. Mac then went and stood over the dead body, still letting the choppa rip.

Then he ran towards the front of the house.

In the front of the house, Jarvis kept firing shot after shot after shot while Rico ducked back inside the car and crawled out of the passenger's side door. He moved towards the trunk of the car and he came up firing.

A bullet caught Jarvis right in the head, splattering his thoughts everywhere. KeeKee stopped screaming when she heard the gunshots cease. Her heart was beating like a bass drum. She pressed her head to the floor and tried to be as quiet as she could while she laid on the floorboard.

Mac was running from the side of the house when he saw Rico, but Rico also saw him. He was putting more bullets in his revolver. Now he rushed the bullet chamber closed and fired at Mac. Mac ducked back against the house and let shots ring from the chopper.

Mac watched him run for the Mustang, so he ran after him. Rico got in the car, letting Mark's body fall all the way out to the ground, as he pulled off with the tires screaming. Mac ran through the yard, sending shots through the car. The whole back window blew out as the car went down the street, looking and moving like a Nascar 500.

PrettyBoy walked from the front door of the house, carrying a black duffel bag over his shoulder. He was rubbing his chest as he walked from the house. He had noticed the duffel bag sitting by the window where Mario had tried to escape from. When he opened it and looked inside, he saw that it was filled with money and he couldn't believe his luck. He just hated that KeeKee had to go through all that she had went through just for him to get this money. He would definitely use this money to make all of their lives better. He thought about all of this as he ambled out of the house.

He saw Mac walking over to somebody laying on the ground, then he noticed that the somebody was Jarvis. He sped up his walk, his heart racing. He knew that it couldn't be good because of how Jarvis's body lay as stiff as a board.

Mac kneeled down and picked up Jarvis's upper body and cradled him in his arms.

"Damn, man, muthafuckas killed him," Mac said with tears running down his face

PrettyBoy stood over him with tears running down his face too, but he couldn't find the words to speak. He just stared at his friend. He couldn't speak the words from his mouth, but he knew right then that he would give all of this money or all of the money in the world to have his friend back. It was written all over his face as water came from his eyes. He didn't have to speak, because his heart had already spoken

"Come on, y'all, we got to go!" KeeKee yelled out of the car's window, breaking the trance. "Come on, the police coming, we got to go."

PrettyBoy snapped out of it and looked up as he heard the approaching police sirens. "Come on, Mac, man, we got to get out of here."

"Damn!" Mac yelled as he got to his feet.

Then they both ran and jumped into the Malibu and pulled off, thinking to themselves, *Damn, my nigga Jarvis gon'...*

***

In the Mustang, Rico picked up his Motorola Nextel phone and hit the two-way radio.

"Grid!" he yelled into the phone. "Grid!" he yelled again while punching the gas pedal to the floor.

"Yo," GridLock answered. "What up?"

"Man, they got Mark," Rico said into the phone.

"What?" GridLock asked, as he wasn't sure he heard correctly.

"They got Mark!" Rico said again.

"What the fuck you mean they got Mark? What happened?" Grid-Lock asked, confused.

"Yo son, it was an ambush. They was waiting on us when we got there!" Rico said while flying down the street in the Mustang. For a while there was no answer, then Rico said, "Yo, what's up, Grid?"

"Yo, I'm here. Get back to the spot. I got something for those muthafuckas," GridLock replied on the other end.

"Alright kid, I'm on my way," Rico shot back before throwing the phone down onto the passenger seat, almost flipping the Mustang as he bent another corner, all gas and no brakes. "Damn...Mark..."

Chapter 26
Paid in full

It was dark outside and the neighborhood of Lantana apartment complex was quiet - all except in the house where PrettyBoy and his crew were.

"Ooohhhh my God, why, why?" Monica cried into Mac's chest as they sat on the living room couch. He held her in his arms with tears in his own eyes as he tried to comfort her. After hearing the news about Jarvis' death, she was devastated, distraught, and in turmoil. Every one of them was also hurt from the loss of their close friend.

"I can't believe this shit!" Mike said. Mike was sitting up in the living room chair with his face in his hands.

PrettyBoy was standing up, walking back and forth like a caged animal. He had his jacket off and the two Desert Eagles swinging from side to side as he walked.

"So what do we do from here?" Mike asked, looking up at Pretty-Boy for his answer.

"I really don't know, shawty. We really ain't got too much to go on," he answered honestly.

"Man, that was them New York niggas," Mac shot back instantly.

"I know it, folk," PrettyBoy confirmed.

"So where them niggas be at?" Mike asked, ready to get some straightening.

"That's what I'm sayin', we don't know," PrettyBoy said, then continued. "KeeKee told me all she knew was that they used to supply Mario. They would meet somewhere in the city, that's it," he finished as they all sat there quiet for a minute.

"Somebody gon' pay for this shit!" Monica blurted out through tears that cascaded down her heartbroken face.

PrettyBoy sat down on the love seat by himself and laid back on the sofa. "Yeah baby, believe that, somebody gon' pay for this shit, Monica. Somebody gon' pay!" he assured with death in his eyes.

***

Later that night, PrettyBoy sat on the bed, still fully dressed. He watched KeeKee as she laid in the bed on her back with the covers pulled up to her chest. She had patches on her face from the beating she took earlier that day. He ogled her as she slept. He took off his shoes, then put his arms around her and leaned over, kissing her on the forehead.

"I love you, baby, and I promise I'll never let anything like this happen to you ever again," he assured in a low and compassionate tone.

"I love you too," KeeKee whispered back, opening her eyes, giving him a weak smile.

PrettyBoy smiled back, elated that his girl was safe. "You alright, baby?"

"Yeah, I'm alright. I'm sorry about what happened,'" she said, struggling to talk.

"Nall, baby, it ain't your fault."

"I should have listened to you and never went back," she admitted, feeling exceedingly bad about all that had transpired.

"It's alright, baby girl, don't you even worry about none of that shit," he replied before giving her another kiss on the cheek as he climbed in the bed with her. He lay there holding her in his arms.

"I love you," said KeeKee.

"I love you too," he said right back to her as their foreplay opened up into a night full of wonderful, exotic, and compassionate lovemaking.

Chapter 27
The start of a new beginning
A few weeks later

At a Longhorn steakhouse restaurant, there weren't many people inside. At a table in the back, four people were just getting settled in at their seats: Monica, PrettyBoy, Mac, and Mike.

Monica was looking a lot better than she was feeling. She wore a purple Baby Phat top and bottom outfit with a pair of black heels. PrettyBoy wore a button down Enyce shirt with dark jeans to match and a pair of custom-made Nike Air Forces. He pulled a chair out from the table so that Monica could have a seat as she approached the table. Mike and Mac sat down in their seats. Mike's arm was finally out of the sling. He had on an Akademik outfit, a black, green, and red T-shirt with a pair of Akademik jeans. Mac was dressed real relaxed with a pair of gray Sean John sweatpants, a white T-shirt, white Air Force 1's, and an Atlanta Braves baseball cap. To him, clothes really didn't matter. He had just lost his closest cousin. They had all just attended Jarvis's funeral a couple of days ago. Now it was PrettyBoy who had come up with this idea to meet and talk. It was cool, because they all really needed to talk.

Mac sat there thinking about Jarvis. How could he not? He was their missing link, their homie, brother, and friend. Jarvis was sent off in style. His funeral was held at a huge church. The whole funeral was done in white, everything from the hundreds of roses that were around his white casket with the white gold rails to his white Armani suit down to his white alligator shoes. The chorus members' robes were white, and all the decorations in the church were white. Even the four stretch Navigators they rented were white. The funeral was talked about all through the streets of Atlanta. It was definitely a major event. Everyone in the clique also wore white too. It was a statement that they were making. Every one of them agreed that it was going to be the only way that they themselves would want to go, if that time ever came, and they knew that the time would come one day because the only thing that life did promise was death. Plus they all felt that Jarvis had a good heart and they knew that he should be somewhere in heaven by now. The funeral had cost $50,000. They felt it was the least they could do since he wouldn't have a chance to enjoy the money.

Just as PrettyBoy and the crew were sitting down at their table, a young waitress walked up. "Hi, my name is Nicole and I'll be your waitress for today," stated the light-skinned slim and very petite girl with a nice smile. "Would you guys like to try today's special?"

"Um, could you give us just a minute?" replied Monica.

"Yeah, sure. Can I get you anything to drink while you decide?" asked the waitress.

"Yeah, let me get a Coca Cola," said PrettyBoy.

"I'll take an Apple Martini." Monica said politely.

"I'll take a Coca Cola too," Mac said.

"Anything you got strong," said Mike, completing the order.

The waitress looked at him and smiled. "Alright then, coming right up." She walked away to fill the orders.

They all started to look at their menus.

"Shit, I already know what I want," Monica said, closing her menu and setting it down on the table.

"I'm going to have to try one of them Big Boy steaks," PrettyBoy said, setting his menu down as well.

"You alright, Mac?" Monica asked, noticing that he hadn't touched his menu.

"Yeah, baby girl, I'm straight. What about you? You alright?" Mac asked, truly feeling some type of way.

"Yeah, baby, I'm good. I just miss Jarvis, that's all," she answered, kinda sad at the thought of his loss.

"We all do," Mike said. "It just don't feel the same."

"For real, man, I know what you mean. I keep thinking he outside in the car or something about to come walking here," PrettyBoy confessed.

"For real, I probably done called his name about fifty times today," confessed Monica, on the verge of tears.

"Yeah, I miss that nigga," Mac said, then Monica reached over and grabbed his hand.

"It seems like just yesterday when we was in middle school and he was playing basketball. That nigga was shining back them when he used to rock that high-ass box," PrettyBoy said with a high laugh as he reminisced.

"Hell yeah, what he used to call that shit? A high right low left," Mike said as they all began to laugh.

"Aw man, I know you didn't go there. You know he used to love that box," said Monica as she laughed as well, feeling the joy of old memories.

"Hell yeah. I remember that time when niggas at school was clowning him about that shit. Boy, that's the first time I saw Jarvis beat the shit out of a nigga," Mac said as he recalled the incident.

Then they all started laughing again. They went on reminiscing about Jarvis for about an hour, remembering all the good times that they had shared together. They talked about when they were in middle school and when they had graduated. They talked until the food came and until they were halfway through with their meal. That's when PrettyBoy felt that it was time to talk to them about why he had really called this meeting.

"Say, I know y'all wondering why I wanted to meet here tonight. Well, I just felt like we needed to talk and get some of this pain off our chest, because I know we all missing Jarvis and plus, we got a lot we need to talk about," PrettyBoy started as everybody at the table shook their heads or gave a gesture to show that they understood and were in agreement. So PrettyBoy went on talking.

"That money we got from the house was $325,000, so now our lives going to be a whole lot different. That's some nice change, but it wasn't worth our nigga Jarvis' life. I'd give anything to have that nigga back and I know y'all feel the same." He looked everybody in their eyes as he continued to talk. "We spent 50 on the funeral, plus his momma got a hundred, so that leaves us with $175. Check this out. We could split it up and we can stop here and just go on living our lives." He paused to see if anybody had anything to say.

For a minute everyone was quiet while they thought things over. They all stared at each other, all lost in their own thoughts.

"Or we can do what we planned and get to this money in a major way," PrettyBoy finished, breaking the silence.

The statement caught all of their attention.

"My nigga, I feel like we done came this far and we could stop now, but then what? Jarvis wouldn't even want it to go down like that, and I can't even see it going down like dat. My nigga would have died for nothing. But then again, it ain't too much we can do to find the other niggas that had something to do with his death, but we can focus on getting our money up and making sure that his name will always and forever be remembered all throughout the streets of the city!" Mike said, and you could tell that every word came from his heart.

"I feel the same way," Monica agreed

"I'm feeling the same way too. I'm ready to make everybody feel us and know that it's our time. I'm ready to fuck the game up," Pretty-Boy announced as though he was ready to take on the world, head first.

"That's what's popping. I'm all in like a poker game!" Mike assured as he rubbed his hands together, ready to get handling business as usual.

"So what's up, Mac? How you feel about it?" PrettyBoy asked, not sure about how Mac felt about the situation.

They all stared at Mac, awaiting his response. He looked at them, making eye contact with each of them. These were his friends -hell, this was his family, he thought. They all could see in his eyes that he was ready - ready to make his impression on the world. Then he spoke.

"Man, let's get this muthafuckin' money!"

And from then on, it was the start of a new beginning.

Chapter 28
Taking it to another level
Six months later

After losing Jarvis, the Mac-11 team all put their minds to bigger and better things. They all decided to go on with the plan. PrettyBoy took his team straight to the top of Atlanta's drug ring. The name Mac-11 started to create a real buzz through the streets of the A.T.L.

Monica handled her end of the bargain by finding good apartments and homes for them to set up shop in, turning the premises into real crack houses. Reinforcement doors were put up on all of the houses, new security windows, heavy duty toilets were installed so they could flush the cocaine with no problem (if need be), plus in every house was a big tub full of acid. With the new doors and windows, they didn't have to worry about the police getting inside the place without a really long struggle, and by then, all the shit would be gon'. Cameras were also installed outside around the place. All the security measures they took helped to eliminate the presence of robbers and the cops, any and all unwanted and unwelcome visitors. They had eleven spots up and running, everywhere from Decatur, Clayton County, Douglasville, East Point, Bankhead, Cascade Road, Cobb County, MLK, Campbelton Road, Adamsville, and Pittsburg.

PrettyBoy and the crew were making more money than they had ever dreamed of. They finally started to experience the finer and more eloquent things in life: expensive cars, homes, and other things that came with being wealthy. PrettyBoy could now do all of the things that he wanted to do for KeeKee. He bought her expensive gifts, took her on week-long cruises, flights overseas and all. They were having the time of their lives.

The crew had gotten together for PrettyBoy's birthday and were in Justin's restaurant in Atlanta that the rapper P. Diddy had opened. They were all dressed up and looking their best. As everyone sat at the large table, Mike was standing to propose a toast.

"I would like to propose a toast," he said with his wine glass raised up to the sky. He wore a black silk Armani long sleeve shirt that had black stripes going down it, with black slacks and black alligator shoes to match. He also was draped in diamonds, looking like a walking chandelier.

Everybody stopped talking to hear what he had to say. Monica was sitting to his right, looking like a goddess, as she wore a forest green silk Prada dress that hung from her shoulders, revealing a little cleavage. She was feeling like a million bucks with all the diamonds hanging from her neck. Across from where Monica was sitting was Mac with a Cuban cigar in his mouth. He was wearing a navy-blue dress shirt with a gray silk tie, navy blue slacks, and a pair of blue and gray alligator square toes. He topped it off with a gray derby hat and diamonds in both ears and on his wrist. At the other end of the table, KeeKee sat next to her man, PrettyBoy. She had on a black charcoal silk dress that clung to her body. It was a short dress that showed her black, curvy thighs. Diamonds were in her ears and around her neck. PrettyBoy wore a black charcoal suit with a dark pink shirt and a gray silk tie with diamond cufflinks. Both he and KeeKee were wearing Armani. PrettyBoy's neck, wrist, and ears were blinged out, lit up like a Christmas tree. In the meantime, everybody raised their glasses.

"For the birthday boy, PrettyBoy James. We all love you, my nigga. We came from the bottom and now we on top. I remember us riding the Marta, but as times got harder, we got smarter, my nigga. I just want you to know that with or without all this shit, you still my nigga for life. I'll give you my lung if you ever need it, my nigga. I love you. And we gon' keep doing this shit for Jarvis," Mike finished, nearly in tears.

"For Jarvis," Mac said, shaking his wine glass farther towards the sky.

"For Jarvis!" all of them said in unison.

"And for us, Mac-11 for life," Mike announced.

"Mac-11!" they all repeated in union as they clicked their glasses together, then Mike took his seat.

Everybody sipped their drinks and had huge smiles on their faces.

"Okay, everybody check this out," PrettyBoy said. "We finally made it to where we wanted to be. Now look, I got a colossal power play in motion. Our Florida connect got a major deal for us, if we can spend right. The deal is, they got a whole truckload coming next month some time. The more we buy, the sweeter the ticket. I want to get a hundred," PrettyBoy informed

Mac whistled at the number he heard.

"Yeah," PrettyBoy said. "If we gon' do it, we gon' do it big." he said as he popped his collar, bossing up as usual.

"But PrettyBoy, you think we gonna be able to cover that shit?" Mike asked from across the table.

"Yeah, we'll be able to cover it if we grind hard in the streets. But we gon' have to really put our muthafuckin' feet down in the city though," PrettyBoy answered with the confidence of a lion.

"How much they want a key?" Mike questioned.

"If we buy a hundred, we can get them for 5," PrettyBoy replied with a devious smile.

"That's five thousand, right?" Mike asked him.

"Yeah." PrettyBoy nodded his head. "This a chance of a lifetime. I ain't tryin' to pass it up."

"Well, let's do it." Mike replied, being vigilant of how sweet this deal really was.

"Let's do it," Mac quickly agreed.

"That's what's up," Monica said, confirming her decision.

KeeKee put her hand on PrettyBoy's arm as he looked at her and said, "Well, say less. It's time to put the hustle to the test."

***

On their way out the restaurant, it was dark and the night was cool. They walked out the restaurant doors and headed towards the cars that were parked side by side in the parking lot. PrettyBoy walked with KeeKee under his arm. Mac and Mike walked out in front of them, and Monica came out last. There was a gray CL500 Mercedes Benz, a black 745 BMW, and a black Benz 600, and all of them were sitting on chrome 20-inch rims. Everyone stepped in front of the cars and gave each other hugs and pounds.

"Alright, my nigga, y'all hold it down," Mac said as he walked to the Benz 600.

"Alright, girl," Monica and KeeKee said as they exchanged hugs, then Monica walked over to the Benz with Mac.

"Y'all niggas be easy," she said to PrettyBoy and Mike as she got into the car and they pulled off.

KeeKee walked over and jumped in passenger side of the Benz CL 500 while Mike and PrettyBoy gave each other pounds, standing outside the cars talking.

"Say, birthday boy, you know we got to do it big tonight. I got a real surprise for you," Mike informed PrettyBoy.

"Oh yeah? That's a bet." PrettyBoy said

"Y'all just go drop the old lady off and when you done, hit me up," Mike told him

"Alright, I'm gon' do that," PrettyBoy said, smiling, thinking to himself, *I love my niggas!*

"Alright now," Mike said as he walked to his BMW 745 with a smile the size of the Pacific Ocean.

PrettyBoy got in his CL500 and pulled off. As the car drifted down the street with ease, KeeKee turned to look at him.

"You had a good time tonight, daddy?" she asked.

"Yeah baby, it was nice. How about you?" he asked her while weaving in and out of traffic.

"Yeah," KeeKee replied, still looking at him.

As PrettyBoy looked at her, he could tell that something was on her mind. "What's up, baby, you got something on your mind?" he asked her, already knowing the truth.

"Did Mike ask you to go somewhere with him tonight?" she asked him.

PrettyBoy laughed. "Yeah, he wants to take me out. KeeKee, you know it's my birthday. He just wants to go out and have a couple of drinks and shit."

"A couple of drinks? Yeah, I bet he do," KeeKee shot back, agitated because she had other plans for them as well.

"Oh, come on now, I know you ain't trippin'," PrettyBoy shot back in disbelief.

"Yeah, lately we don't really spend enough time together and plus with this new thing you about to do, it's going to really take a lot of your time. It ain't just about it's supposed to be about us. I don't know why you want to push this thing any further. We doing alright now, PrettyBoy," she complained.

PrettyBoy just sat back and thought for a minute as he handled the wheel like a champ. "Alright, I'm going to call Mike and tell him I'm going to chill tonight."

"Alright, but you still ain't said nothing about this other thing." KeeKee said, still pushing the issue.

"KeeKee, baby, look, this is my chance to really get straight and I ain't about to pass it up," PrettyBoy said as though it was final.

KeeKee just stared out of the window, lost in thought as she felt an eerie feeling in her gut that spelled disaster.

Trai'Quan

Chapter 29
Six Flags

The next morning, Mac was at this bachelor pad in Buckhead, getting ready to start his day. It was a two-bedroom apartment with black leather furniture. He had the ideal spot for a guy his age, everything a young man could dream of, from the entertainment center, to the bar he had in the living room. His bedroom looked like a jungle due to all of the animal carpets he had. The place was very nice. Mac had phenomenal taste. He laid in the bed as he slowly began to awake, stretching and yawning while he regained his eyesight. He noticed that he wasn't alone in his queen-sized bed. He looked over at the light-skinned woman with curly long black hair lying next to him.

Damn, she almost look like Ashanti, Mac thought to himself, as he stared at the broad. Then he began to smile as he thought about the night before. *She was a freak too*, he thought as the memory set in.

He then slowly pulled the sheets back and stood from the bed. He had on a pair of blue silk boxers and he was about to make his way to the bathroom when he noticed something laying on the floor from the corner of his eye. Damn, it wasn't something; it was someone. It was another woman! She was a brown-skinned female with brown and blond braids in her hair and she was stupid thick. The girl just laid there on the floor with her legs wide open, and she was naked except for a pair of red panties. Shit, he had forgotten about her. How could he have forgotten her after the show she and her friend had performed? The bitch could eat pussy better than him. Hell, probably better than any man. PrettyBoy really didn't know what he had missed last night. It was amazing how freaky a person could get after taking some ecstasy.

That X is the shit! Mike thought as he went in the bathroom and started to wash his face. Then he got his toothbrush, loaded it up with Crest extra mint plus whitening, and started to brush his teeth. Just as he finished, he heard the ring of his cell phone. He walked back into the bedroom, picked up the phone from the night stand, and answered.

"Yo, what's the bizness?"

"What's up, nigga?" PrettyBoy's voice shot back through the receiver.

"What's happening, pimpin'?" Mac said, surprised to hear from him this early. "My nigga, I was just thinking about your ass, nigga."

"Oh yeah," PrettyBoy said with a laugh.

"Yeah. I was thinking about how KeeKee got your ass whipped," Mac shot back as they both laughed together.

"Fuck you, nigga!" PrettyBoy joked.

"Nall, you should have been over here fucking these two freaky-ass hoes I got over here with me right now," Mac corrected him.

"Say what?" PrettyBoy asked, thinking to himself, *Is this nigga for real?*

"Yeah nigga, theses bitches got on that X and took that shit to another level," Mac said. "Shit, I'm like T.I.P. bussin' in they faces while they kiss they partners with it in they faces," Mac joked.

PrettyBoy just laughed at his partna as he knew that he was most definitely feeling himself.

"But on the real, PrettyBoy, we need to invest in that X, my nigga. That's what's up," Mac said, getting serious as a heart attack.

"Shit, we might need to do that. We'll see what we can work out. I know it's some money in that shit," PrettyBoy agreed.

"Hell yeah, everybody fucking with that shit," Mac said. "I know some people we might can fuck with."

"Alright, bet, check on it and see what's up," PrettyBoy said as the dollar signs flashed through his head.

"That's a bet, I'll do that. But what up though? Where you headed this early?" Mac asked as he sat on the bed. When he sat down, the girl on the bed started to wake up.

"Man, I'm about to hit this Six Flags spot with KeeKee," PrettyBoy said with a half-smile.

"You talking about Six Flags the amusement park?" Mac asked, sounding surprised. Mac raised his voice and the girl on the floor woke up.

"Yeah, man, I'm gon' go out there and have a good time with my baby," PrettyBoy replied.

"I feel you, my nigga," Mac said, not even noticing the girl crawling on all fours making her way over towards him with her titties hanging and swinging everywhere. Once she got to him, she reached inside his boxers while Mac listened to PrettyBoy talk on the other end.

"Man, you want to get with one of your shawties and hit the park with us?" PrettyBoy was saying, but Mac couldn't hear him because the girl that was on the bed had sat up and draped her arms around his shoulders as she rubbed his chest and kissed on his neck. The other girl took his dick to her mouth and went to sucking on him like he was her favorite lollipop.

"Damn, baby," Mac moaned as he dropped the phone on the bed. Then he laid back on the bed as PrettyBoy hollered through the receiver.

The girl on the bed went to kissing all over his chest, while playing in her pussy, moaning out in ecstasy. Mac grabbed the phone.

"Baby, we got to get the X!" he reassured PrettyBoy as both women took flight on him.

PrettyBoy laughed. "Alright, playboy, I'ma fuck wit'cha. Hit me up later," he said before hanging up.

"Holla!" Mac said as he threw the phone across the room, grabbing one of the li'l sexy bitches by the back of the head, shoving his dick in and out of her mouth at top notch speed, thinking to himself, *Damn, this li'l mouth dumb stupid wet. We got to get a plug on dat X!*

***

Later that same day, KeeKee and PrettyBoy were at Six Flags, really enjoying each other. They were so in love that they looked like the perfect couple, as though they didn't have a problem or any cares in the world.

PrettyBoy was thinking to himself that this was definitely what he was missing. The park was wonderful. All types of rides, amazing roller coasters that made you scream for your life. They had rode the Batman, the Superman, and some rides where lovers rode through a haunted house. It was great. They both were having fun just being together.

PrettyBoy was at a tall basketball goal shooting shot after shot, tryin' to win KeeKee a basketball. He had missed about ten shots already. A small crowd had gathered around to watch. Hell, with the game costing $3 a shot, he could had bought her 10 basketballs by now. But that didn't matter. He had to win his girl one of those balls.

"Baby, I'm going to hit this one right here?" PrettyBoy said as he positioned the ball in his hands, getting ready to take the shot. He concentrated, locked his eyes on the basket, then shot. The ball hit the rim then rolled out. He had again. "Damn," PrettyBoy said, still determined to hit the shot.

The crowd cheered.

"Aw baby, come on, you got to hit one for me now," KeeKee said, encouraging her man with a sexy and seductive smile.

"Baby, I got you," PrettyBoy assured, pulling out his bankroll. He turned to the man behind the counter of the game. "Give me ten more shots," he told him with the cash in his hands.

"Alright," the man replied as he took the $30. Then he gave PrettyBoy another ball and the crowd began to cheer him on. The man behind the counter was an older man, probably in his forties. He liked to see the younger kids in their relationships. It made him think of his old days, when he, too, was young and in love. "Alright now, son, you better make one of these, because if I had a pretty li'l thang like you got here, boy, I would make all ten," the man joked with PrettyBoy, causing KeeKee to blush uncontrollably.

"Oh, see now, you tryin' to take my girl," PrettyBoy said joking back with the man, causing the crowd to laugh as they all enjoyed the show.

"Okay, I tell you what, keep them balls coming," PrettyBoy said, now motivated and exceedingly determined to get the ball (one of them) into the basket.

Then he shot the ball. He missed again - in fact, he missed seven shots in a row. Then he hit the last three, yelling, "How you like them apples!"

The crowd celebrated and clapped as though he had just won a real championship game. KeeKee and PrettyBoy got their three basketballs for winning, then they began to walk through the amusement park. The park was crowded. Kids ran past family groups walking together, and couples in love walked about holding hands, kissing, hugging, and truly enjoying one another.

PrettyBoy dribbled one of the basketballs as he walked and Kee-Kee walked beside him holding the other two as if they were worth a million dollars.

"You big show off," KeeKee said.

"What?" PrettyBoy said, pretending not to have heard her.

"You heard me, nigga," KeeKee said, joking with him.

"Who you talking to, girl?" he said, smiling as he ran up to her face to face.

They stopped walking and stood there, just staring into each other's eyes.

"You, you show off," she said, still standing her ground, extremely aroused by her man

"You like that shit," he shot back as he kissed her softly and passionately, sticking his tongue deep into her mouth, exploring the tunnel behind her lips.

She smiled and said. "And you like that."

They slowly let go, both trying to catch their breath.

PrettyBoy laughed as they went back to walking again. Then he slapped her on the ass dumb stupid hard.

"Ow!" KeeKee yelled. "Boy!"

"Nall, I like that," he said, laughing .

He took off running with KeeKee chasing him through the park, screaming, "I'ma beat your ass, PrettyBoy!"

***

It was getting late in the day and they were just getting off a roller coaster. This particular roller coaster took your picture while you were on the ride. KeeKee was a little shook up from the trip. PrettyBoy walked in front of her laughing as they made their way to the counter, where a big TV screen was divulging the pictures from the ride.

"Come on, baby, they about to show our picture," PrettyBoy informed as he held out his arm and threw it around KeeKee's neck.

"I don't even want to see this," she said, causing PrettyBoy to smile. "Boy, I don't know why the hell I let you talk me into riding this roller coaster." He busted out laughing at her. She hit him in the chest. "Why you laughing at me?"

"Baby, you should have saw how you was looking," he shot back through laughs.

"Forget you!" she yelled, half-laughing herself.

"100K, baby, there we go!" he said as he saw their picture pop up on the screen. In the picture, PrettyBoy held on to the rail inside the roller coaster with one hand and the other arm was around KeeKee, while she held her head down in his chest with her eyes closed.

PrettyBoy couldn't help but to burst out laughing, once again thinking to himself, *This girl here too much. But I love the hell out of her, straight up!*

Chapter 30
This is the life

The next morning in a white huge house in Buckhead, where the most prosperous and wealthy people lived in Atlanta, KeeKee was sitting at the kitchen table alone. It was KeeKee's and PrettyBoy's new place. KeeKee said that it was the house of her dreams. KeeKee sat at the Italian made table in a white robe with nothing on underneath. Pretty-Boy was making his way down the stairs just as she got up to get a cup of coffee. When he walked in the kitchen, she was standing at the counter with her back to him. She was just starting the coffee maker. Pret-tyBoy wore a white Akademik velour jogging suit with a pair of cus-tom-made Air Force 1's. She didn't even notice him as he came into the kitchen. He walked over to her and grabbed her around the waist, then pushed up against her as close as he could.

"Uhhh…good morning," he said to her. "Yeah, you wore me out last night," he said into her ear as his hand slid inside her robe. He slowly kissed her on the neck as his hand cuffed one of her breasts.

"Umm," she moaned while throwing her head, back enjoying her man's gentle, but passionate touch. PrettyBoy continued to massage her nipples and kiss her neck, allowing his nature to rise. "Damn, baby," KeeKee moaned, feeling herself getting wet. Then she turned around and threw her arms around him and kissed him. They kissed for a while as she did her best to catch her breath.

"I got to go handle some business," he said, quickly fixing his cloths.

"See, PrettyBoy, this exactly what I'm talking about," she argued.

"Baby, don't start tripping," he shot back, giving her a peck on the lips as he reached into his pocket and pulled out a big ole bankroll rapped in rubber bands. "Here, go to the mall and get something sexy to wear for me tonight. I'll be home early," he informed with dope boy swag.

KeeKee took the money and smiled as she put it in her robe pocket. PrettyBoy kissed her hard and deep.

This is why I love this man so much, she thought as she kissed him back. He grabbed her and sat her up on the counter. He then started to kiss her breasts, then her neck, then he worked his way to her mouth as he pulled his dick out from his pants. He slowly went deep inside of her.

"Ooohh," she moaned as she slid back against the counter as far as she could. But she couldn't get away.

***

Later that day, KeeKee walked through Lennox Mall, trying to buy it all. It was a two-story mall that stayed packed with plenty of people. She wore Apple Bottom jeans, a sky blue top that showed a little cleavage, and sky-blue open toe heels, with blue and white ribbons in her long ponytail. Her hands were full of bags as she walked through the mall. She made her way to the food court section of the mall with a variety of smells enticing her.

Damn, I'm hungry, she thought to herself as she looked around trying to decide what she want to eat. "Damn, this muthafucka crowded." She stood there looking at the lines at every food restaurant. "But a bitch got to eat." She went to set down her bags at a nearby chair. She had decided on a pizza place. She slowly made her way over to the line and began to wait. She was standing there looking at the menu that they had positioned up, minding her own business, when someone walked up and stood beside her so she turned to see who it was. *Damn*, KeeKee thought as she looked over and saw the handsome man standing next to her. He was looking right at her. He had light brown eyes. He was about 6 feet tall, 170 pounds , light brown skin, with a mouth full of platinum teeth smiling right at her. He had on a gray hoodie, some big baggy jeans, and a pair of gray Timbs with a gray fittie cap. The nigga was thugged out.

"How you doing, miss lady?" he asked her.

"Hey," KeeKee said, blushing just a little.

"I'm Tay. I just had to come introduce myself. You wearing the hell out them jeans, baby," Tay complimented while looking KeeKee over attentively.

KeeKee couldn't help but to blush and laugh. "Thank you," she managed to say, feeling her temperature rising.

"So what's your name?" he asked.

"My name's KeeKee," she replied with an innocent smile.

"So what are you, KeeKee, a model or something?" Tay asked, tryna butter KeeKee up even more.

"Oh, come on, I guess you about to spit your game at me now." KeeKee laughed, peeping the punchlines.

"Nall, I ain't' gon' spit no game, because then I'll be wasting both of our time. I think we both too old for games," he said as she stared at him.

"I don't know, you look kind of young though. How old are you?"

Tay smiled, "Old enough, old enough, ma."

KeeKee smiled, knowing that he had to be young.

"Check this out, shawty, you with somebody?" he asked. "Nall," Tay answered his own question. "Because if you was here with a nigga, you wouldn't even be talking to me. I tell you what. Why don't we get this food and sit down and get to know each other a little better?" he asked, hoping that she wouldn't deny his request.

"How you know I want to get to know you, Tay?" KeeKee questioned him with her hands on her hips, slightly rolling her neck.

"Ma, unless your eyes are lying to me and your brain is deceiving you, you want to. Believe me you want to, shawty."

"Tay, I got a man," KeeKee replied finally.

He just smiled and reached into his pocket and pulled out a card. "Here go my number. You think about it, alright?" he said as he held out the card.

KeeKee took it.

"Alright, KeeKee, I'ma holla," he said, then walked off as nonchalant as he could be.

She watched him as he walked away.

"Miss, can I help you?" asked someone working behind the counter of the pizza joint.

"Oh shit" KeeKee mumbled as she had forgotten all about her pizza. She was the only one in line waiting. She walked up to the counter to place her order. She then put Tay's card into her pocket, not even thinking about ever calling him.

Trai'Quan

Chapter 31
Got to be more careful

The gentlemen's club was an upscale Atlanta strip club. Inside were some of the best-looking women that the city had to offer. The club was a real hot spot. All of the ballers and big money spenders visited the club frequently. Tonight was no different. It was Saturday night, and the place was off the chain.

Mac and Mike came through the doors with quite a big entourage. There were nine of them in all. All of them wore black leather jackets, like school jackets, that had Mac-11 on the back in silver. They looked like a thugged-out football team as they walked inside the club with Mac and Mike leading the pack.

The DJ was playing 50 Cent's song "Just a Little Bit." He gave a shout out to the crew as they walked through the place.

"Ok, yeah, ladies, Mac-11 in this muthafucka tonight! All y'all stingy niggas better pull your money out now!" the DJ said as Mike and the crew made their way over to a couple of tables in the corner.

Mike stood up. "Yeah, baby, Mac-11 up in this bitch tonight. That's the bizness! Let's get some dranks up in this muthafucka!" he yelled over the music, ready to turn up.

A sexy dark-skinned woman with a short skirt on ran over with a tray in her hand. "Hey Mike, what can I get for y'all fellas tonight?" she asked with a flirtatious smile and voice.

"Look, baby, get me two bottles of Cristal and get my niggas whatever they want," he said, pulling out a dumb bank roll. Then he peeled off six hundred dollar bills and gave them to the broad as the rest of the clique started shouting orders. Before long, the Mac-11 clique had most of the ladies in the club headed to their tables.

"What's up, Mike baby?" a brown-skinned fox named Cinnamon said, walking to Mike's table as he sat down.

"What's the bizness, li'l momma?" Mike said.

"Shit, you. You gon' let a bitch dance for you?" Cinnamon asked as all the other fellas stared at her 34-22-39 shape.

"Hell yeah, take that shit off," Mike ordered as he spread a wad of money out in his hands, thumbing through the check with ease.

Cinnamon complied with no problem, dropping her clothes to the floor as she danced to the Ying Yang Twins and Jackio's song. "Drop that pussy, now roll with it, roll with it…"

The music played, turning the club all the way up as all types of other bad, half-naked bitches ran over to their tables. Before long, everybody had a girl butt ass naked dancing in front of them.

Cinnamon was just getting warmed up as she dropped her ass up and down in front of Mike, then stopped and started making her ass vibrate, then she made it clap for him.

"Oh shit, baby. That's what I'm talking about!" Mike yelled as he made it rain on the stripper.

She then turned to face him and threw her leg on his chair as she leaned up and whispered in his ear. "Daddy you gon' beat this pussy up after the club closes?" she asked him.

"Girl, I'll beat that pussy up right here," Mike shot back meaning every word.

Cinnamon started laughing as she leaned back and gave him a view of her wet and sweaty juice box. She was hairy too, and Mike liked that. He stuck one of his fingers inside her as she threw her hips back and forth.

"Ummm," she moaned in ecstasy.

He smiled, took his finger out, and held it up while he looked at her. She learned down and sucked her juices off his finger.

"Oooh, you nasty," Mike said with a smile.

She smiled back, saying, "You ain't seen nothing yet!"

Mac was sitting by Mike, but he was too busy watching the black Amazon beauty he had dancing in front of him. "Hold up, baby," Mac told her. "I'll be back."

Then he got up and made his way to the bathroom. He walked inside the restroom and took a leak in one of the stalls.

"Yo, son, that bitch is crazy," someone said as they walked into the bathroom.

"Don, the bitch was gripping my shit like she wanted to rip a nigga shit off, kid, for real," Mac heard a second person say as he finished the toilet.

When he walked out of the stall, he saw the two cats that were talking. One had his back to him, at the urinal pissing, and the other one was at the sink, looking in the mirror.

"What up, Don?" said the dude at the sink when Mac walked up to wash his hands.

"Yo, man I fucking love these Georgia bitches, man," Rico said as he finished taking a leak and turned around to walk to the sink. He was wearing a too big red fitty cap, red hoodie, blue jeans, and red Timberland boots. He walked up to the sink. Mac looked up and they locked eyes.

Mac didn't waste any time. He turned around and caught Rico with a right hook in the jaw. Then all hell broke loose in the bathroom. Rico went down hard, but as he tried to get back up, Mac ran over and kicked him in the head. Rico's partner, Q-Tip, rushed Mac into the stalls. Q-Tip was a skinny Puerto Rican. He wore a white T-shirt, a blue leather jacket and some blue jeans, and a pair of brown Timbs. He almost had Mac inside the stall, but Mac wrestled with him and slammed him to the ground. Q-Tip was no match for him.

But by then Rico had gotten to his feet and had caught Mac with a punch to the head. Mac stumbled back, dazed for a minute, until he finally got control over himself again. He shook the punch off and ducked another wild left Rico threw. He then caught Rico with a right hook, then a left, then a right, then another left, then another right, knocking him out cold. Buddy was asleep. Q-Tip had grabbed the beer bottle he had from the sink and brought it crashing down on Mac's head, almost dropping him to one knee. Glass flew everywhere. Blood leaked from a gash in his head as Mac jumped back to his feet and wouldn't allow himself to hit the ground. Q-Tip swung the broken glass at his face, but he moved his head back just in time.

"Yeah, what up, kid!" Q-Tip yelled as they squared off.

Mac rushed at him with a kick, catching him right in the stomach, just as he swung the bottle and missed. Q-Tip bent over when the kick landed. Mac then caught him with a left hook and a right uppercut, knocking him out, putting him to sleep right beside his mans and them.

"Y'all pussy-ass niggas can't fuck with me!" he yelled, spitting on Q-Tip as he lay on the floor completely unconscious. Then Mac got himself together and walked out.

Just as he was walking out, Rico was getting up. Rico saw the broken bottle on the floor and grabbed it and ran out behind Mac. Mac was walking through the club, tryin' to go tell Mike what had just gone down in the bathroom, when he heard someone running up behind him. He turned around ready to fight, but it was too late. Rico brought the broken bottle down right on Mac's neck. Blood squirted everywhere.

The place broke out in screams. Mike jumped from his seat to see what was up. Rico stood over Mac as he laid on the floor bleeding and coughing up blood. He was shaking like a fish out of water.

"Now what up, you bitch-ass nigga!" Rico yelled down at him belligerently.

Mike saw this and rushed Rico before he even knew what hit him. He went down with Mike on top of him. Mike pounded blow after blow to his face, then he got up and stomped him to sleep literally. The rest of the Mac-11 crew ran over and commenced to beating the shit out of Rico.

The club's bouncers ran over and tried to break up the fight. Three of Rico's partners had also run over and jumped in the fight. It turned into a full-fledged brawl. The bouncers went to bounce people up out of the club, throwing people out on their asses. When Mike got outside of the club, he ran to his black Escalade truck with chrome 24-inch rims and black tinted windows. All of his boys were by the other two trucks parked beside him. They were two black Denali trucks with chrome 24's and black tinted windows also.

"Wassup, Mike, we gon' wet these niggas ass up or what, my nigga!" one of his li'l homies yelled that was standing with the crowd around the trucks.

Mike didn't say nothing as he walked to the trunk of the Escalade and popped it open. He took off his jacket and put on a black hoody sweater.

"Nall, y'all niggas go head and dip. They about to come out of the club in a minute, and when they do, I'm about to light this bitch up like the fourth of July," he said as he picked up twin Glock 40s and put them in his waist.

"Nall, folk, we gon' help murk these bitch-ass niggas," another one of his homies insisted.

"Man, get in the muthafuckin' trucks and pull off!" Mike yelled with his adrenaline pumping, nothing but murder and homicide thru his veins.

"But man, I think them niggas done killed Mac. Man, fuck that, I'ma——" the boy was about to finish, but Mike cut him off.

"Get in the muthafuckin' truck. I got this shit," Mike demanded, not taking no for an answer.

They all reluctantly got in the trucks and pulled off.

Mike pulled the hoody over his head and walked towards the club. He saw Rico and two other dudes coming out. One was Q-Tip. They were walking in a hurry. As soon as they got in the parking lot, Mike walked through the crowd that was at the door and pulled out the two Glock 40s.

He hit Rico and Q-Tip in the chest. The other dude tried to run. He caught him in the back with two quick shots.

People were screaming and running, as the shots had everyone petrified.

Mike walked up to the bodies and shot each of them one time in the head while they were on the ground sprawled in their own blood. He did it fast with no hesitation

"Drop the muthafuckin' gun!" he heard a voice yelling.

Mike turned to the voice and there was a bouncer holding a gun pointed right at him. Mike let off shots at him. The bouncer shot back as Mike took off running.

Mike made it to his truck and jumped in. The bouncer ran out to the street, tryin' to run beside the truck as it swerved through the parking lot.

Boom! Boom!

The bouncer shot as the truck shot past, jumped over the curb, and out into the street. Mike heard the sirens and saw the police and ambulance as they flew past him on their way to the club.

"Damn, I hope my nigga ain't dead," Mike said as he mashed the gas in the truck trying, to do the whole dash.

Chapter 32
It's an all-white affair

At a big white church in East Point, GA, there was a funeral going on. Cars of all makes and models were out lining the streets. The church was called Wings of Faith Ministries. It was an all-black church. The preacher was giving a sermon in the pulpit, standing over the white casket, that was propped up on the floor beneath. Mac's body lay inside with an all-white Armani suit and tie, draped in diamonds.

"For the body is only temporary," the preacher preached.

In the front row sat Mac's family, who all wore white and were shedding tears of joy, sorrow, and pain.

In the second row, Mike sat in a white Sean John suit, white shirt and tie, and white Gators. Next to him sat a beautiful young lady also wearing all white. Across from them, in the other row of pews on the front row, sat Monica with Mac's mother. His mother wore a white dress with a big white hat and some shades. Monica had on a white Dolce and Gabbana dress, with a matching jacket, and a pair of Gucci shades. She held Mac's mom in her arms as she wept.

"For this life has not been meant to last forever by the creator!" the preacher said.

In the back of the church sat PrettyBoy and KeeKee. They were in all white also. PrettyBoy wore Armani. KeeKee wore a Gucci dress and Gucci shades.

"It's your soul that needs to be right with God! Because your soul is what lasts forever," said the preacher as the churchgoers said, "Amen."

PrettyBoy started to zone out as he listened to the preacher. He started to think of all the years that he had spent with Mac. *Damn, why my nigga had to die, God?* he thought to himself, completely heartbroken.

KeeKee reached over and placed her hand on his hand, as if she knew what he was thinking.

"God said, for the punishment of sin is death," the preacher went on ,preaching a sermon that touched many hearts and souls as PrettyBoy just stared out into space.

KeeKee broke the silence. "Baby, who is that girl Mike sitting with?" she asked.

PrettyBoy looked. "Oh, that's them twins he and Mac used to mess with," he answered stoically.

KeeKee looked over there, surprised. "Twins?" she asked, still looking.

"Yeah, baby," he said back.

KeeKee then noticed that it was two girls, one on each side of Mike. They looked exactly the same and were wearing the exact same thing. "Damn," she muttered under her breath.

Then the preacher said, "Now we'll have a number from our choir while everyone pays their last respects."

People started to form a line. The choir stood up and began to sing P. Diddy and Faith Evans' song. "I'll be missing you... Every step I take, every move I make..." they sang as one by one, people viewed the body. KeeKee and PrettyBoy remained seated and watched everyone else.

Mac's mother got to the casket and fainted. Monica had to hold her up until some people helped carry her away. Monica came back and stood over Mac's body and started to cry.

"Damn, boy, why you have to go and get yourself killed? I love you, Mac. I promise I'm gon' get them niggas that did this shit to you." Monica bent over and kissed his cheek. "I love you, Mac," she said through tears as she walked off.

PrettyBoy and KeeKee watched as Mike and the twins made their way to the casket.

"Baby, I'm so sorry about what happened to Mac. When do you think it's going to stop?" KeeKee turned and said to PrettyBoy with desperation in her voice.

He looked at her, asking, "What gon' stop? What you mean, baby?"

"All this - the beef, the drugs, the killing. I don't want to see you in one of these caskets over this bullshit!" KeeKee replied with anger.

"Look, baby, now ain't the time for this shit," he said, frustrated, and really no in the mood to have this type of discussion.

"Well, when is?" snapped KeeKee, not hearing nothing he said.

"Not right now!" he shot back, looking as if he was completely addled.

KeeKee looked into his eyes and said, "I'm sorry baby." Then she kissed him on the cheek.

"It's all good, baby girl," PrettyBoy replied

"I just don't want nothing to happen to you," She said in a dejected voice.

"Baby, ain't nothing going to happen to me."

"You promise?" she asked quizzically.

"I promise." He kissed her again on her soft and beautiful lips as they held hands and watched Mike at the casket.

Mike was talking to Mac. "My nigga, I killed them pussy-ass niggas that night. I'm sorry, baby. If I was on point, you wouldn't have died. Forgive me, bro. My nigga, as long as I live, I live for us! As long as I breathe, I breathe for you. I love you, boy, and I'm going to miss you. We gon' do this shit for you, my nigga, in a major way. Here, man." Mike reached into his suit jacket and pulled the two Glock 40s out from their holsters and laid them inside the casket. "These for you. Them the ones I used. Take them to the grave with you, my nigga, so you can rest in peace. Nigga, you was a gangsta, so we gon' bury you like one. One luv, baby. We gon' keep it movin'," Mike finished as he leaned in the casket and kissed Mac's forehead.

The girls leaned over and kissed Mac and hugged him. Then they all walked off. On their way out of the church, they stopped by Pretty-Boy's row.

"Say, we ridin' together to the gravesite?" Mike asked him.

"Yeah, fo' sho', my nigga," PrettyBoy answered. "We need to talk anyway."

"Bet," Mike replied as he walked out.

PrettyBoy got up and made his way to the casket, stopping dead in his tracks. He stood there for a while. "Mac, I'm going to miss you, baby boy," he whispered as a tear rolled down his cheek. "You was always like a brother to me." Then he put his hand on the casket. "I'll make sure that your legacy lives on through me. Me and Mike gon' hold you down." Then he wiped his face. "Man, this shit just too much. First Jarvis, then you. I can't even believe this shit. My nigga, we gon' miss y'all niggas. It just ain't gon' be the same no more. I was thinking about getting out the game folk, but I don't know. Man, I feel like that's going against everything we worked so hard to build. It's like I see death coming, and I'm tryin' to bitch up and run from the shit. I feel like, that wouldn't even be fair to you, my nigga, you or Jarvis. Because y'all died for the life we live and now, I'm tryin' to cheat and get out the game, to save my life." Tears ran down his face. He wiped his face with his white handkerchief from his breast pocket. "Nall, fuck that shit. Nigga, I'm gon' ride for you. I'm gon' fuck the game up for you and Jarvis. Can't nobody eat but us. Mac-11, my nigga, until I die. And if death do find me... fuck it, so be it! I love you, my nigga. Rest in peace," PrettyBoy remonstrated as he bent down and kissed Mac on the head. He then reached into his pocket and pulled out a large roll of money and threw it into the casket and walked off.

As he made his way to the pew where KeeKee was sitting, he heard a lot of commotion outside.

"Bitch, I don't know who you think you is!" someone was yelling outside.

Then someone inside the church yelled. "They out there fighting!"

The few people that were left inside ran out to see what was going on.

"What the fuck! Come on, baby," PrettyBoy said to KeeKee as he ran out the doors of the church.

"Why the fuck you try to play me, muthafucka?" a brown-skinned girl was yelling in Mike's face. "Who the fuck is these bitches?" she screamed at him, talking about the twins Mike had standing beside him.

"Bitch, you better calm your muthafuckin' ass down," Mike shot back at her.

"Nigga, what? I'll beat——" the girl said as she hauled off and hit one of the twins. "Bitch...you...fucking...with...my...man...bitch," the girl said while hitting the twin and pulling her hair with the other hand.

Mike tried to break it up, but the other twin rushed the girl.

"Bitch! Oh hell nall," she said as she went to raining blows on the girl's head.

The girl's name was Kim, one of Mike's many girlfriends. She had been at the funeral watching Mike the whole time, just waiting for a chance to confront him.

"Hold up, y'all bitches chill out. This my muthafuckin' nigga funeral!" Mike yelled while tryin' to break them up, but it was too late, because it had already become a full-fledged fight and it was starting to get ugly. Kim had knocked one of the twins down and had turned around to take care of the other one. She caught the twin with a hard right haymaker. Blood started to run from the girl's nose. The twin began to scream and held her face with her hands.

"Yeah, bitch, I beat both y'all bitchs' ass! Maybe next time, y'all bitches will think twice before fucking with another bitch's man, bitch!" Kim yelled at her in revulsion.

PrettyBoy walked up just about that time and so did Monica. "Kim, you need to take your muthafuckin' ass home, bitch. Get up out of here with that bullshit!" Mike said, really fed up with her now.

"Ooohhh, muthafucka, you want to take up for your little bitches, you muthafuckin'…" Then she ran up and started swinging on Mike, but before she knew it, she was being pulled back exceedingly hard by the shirt. She spun around.

"Uh-uh, come here, bitch!" Monica said and caught the girl right in the chin with a real manly punch.

Kim fell to the ground and was knocked out cold.

"Ooooooohhhh!" said the crowd.

"Damn!" someone yelled, "she knocked her ass out!"

"I know that bitch, didn't think she was gon' come up in my folks' shit, with that bullshit," Monica said, really feeling herself.

"Y'all get her up out of here," PrettyBoy said to the fellas that were picking Kim up off the ground.

"Take shawty to the hospital," Mike said to his little homies that were out there, referring to the twin with the nosebleed. The other twin was comforting her.

KeeKee, PrettyBoy, Mike and Monica made their way to the car.

"That's fucked up, Mike. Real fucked up. If you gon' have all them bitches, at least keep them in check," Monica said with an attitude as they got to the white Lincoln Continental.

"Yeah, Mike, you know that shit shouldn't have even happened here," PrettyBoy agreed.

"Man, the bitch crazy," Mike said as they got inside the white car with suicide doors and chrome 24-inch rims.

Mike drove with Monica in the passenger seat. PrettyBoy and Kee-Kee sat in the back.

"Damn, Monica knocked that bitch out," PrettyBoy said, causing all of them to laugh.

"I knew you loved me," Mike joked with Monica.

"Boy, please," she shot back as she hit him.

They all laughed some more as Mike cranked up the car. They pulled off with the system banging Maxwell's song "A Woman's Worth".

"I should be cryin', but I just can't let it go..."

Chapter 33
Some things just don't change

The next morning, PrettyBoy and KeeKee house in Buckhead. Pretty-Boy sat on a futon in the middle of the bedroom floor. He was playing the PlayStation 4 that was hooked up to the 6-inch flat screen TV that was mounted to the wall. He had his shirt off with his platinum chain hanging down to his belly button. He also wore a pair of blue and white And-1 basketball shorts and And-1 sneakers to match, plus a white headband on his head. He looked like a real athlete while sitting there playing John Madden 2005 football. KeeKee was sitting on the bed painting her toenails. She had on a gray sports bra with matching spandex shorts. Her hair was in two large ponytails, wrapped in gray and white ribbons.

"Dat nigga can't hold me!" PrettyBoy yelled at the TV. "Who runs this shit? Huh? Huh? Me, that's who," he said, tryin' to sound like Scarface.

"Damn, nigga, you act like you know what you doing over there," KeeKee joked with him

"Oh, I know you ain't talking, Pippi Longstocking," he joked back, still caught up in his game.

"Ooohh," KeeKee laughed. "You want to go there, Pretty Ricky?"

PrettyBoy laughed. "What, you want to see me or something?"

"You ain't said nothing," she shot back.

"Alright, now don't be crying when ya ass be doing some pushups and sit-ups after I get thru draggin' your ass," boasted PrettyBoy.

"Nigga, your ass the one gon' be doing some pushups and sit-ups. Matter fact, I'm gon' help you keep that shit right," she said as she got up from the bed. She stood beside him and looked down at him. "What up?" she asked.

"Well, let that be the reason," he said, then reset the game.

She stood close to him, looking down into his eyes. PrettyBoy looked at her, admiring her shape and curves. She noticed his accolade and smiled.

"Girl, you better sit your li'l sexy ass down before I say fuck the game and just fuck da hell outta you!" shot PrettyBoy.

"Nigga, I'm about to beat your ass," she said, laughing as she sat down right between his legs and grabbed the other controller.

"Ok, now sixty pushups and sit-ups a game?" she consulted.

"Run it, li'l buddy, you ain't said nothing," he shot back as he kissed her on the neck.

"Nall, don't try to break my concentration," she joked just before they picked their teams and made it do what it do ...

KeeKee held herself up in the pushup position.

"32...33...34...huh...35...uh...60, baby," she said while getting up.

"Oh hell nall. You cheating. Aw man." PrettyBoy was laughing as he came out of the bathroom with a T-shirt thrown over his shoulder.

KeeKee was breathing hard and had worked up a little sweat. She held her hands on her hips, tryin' to catch her breath. "Shit, I already did 130, nigga," she said, smiling. "Baby, where you about to go?" she asked.

"I got some bizness I got to go handle. I'm going to meet this nigga at Fulton Industrial at the Summit Hotel. He want to get 5fiveblocks. He willing to pay the high, so I gots to get this money, baby."

"So when you coming back?"

"I don't know, baby. I'll call you on your cell."

"You don't know!" she reiterated with an attitude.

"Gotdamn, man, don't start that shit today," he snapped.

"What the hell you mean don't start!" she said, raising her voice.

"See, there you go. I ain't got time for this shit. Look, I'll holla at you," PrettyBoy said, walking out of the bedroom with great velocity.

KeeKee followed him down the stairs. "This the shit I be talking about. How you just gon' walk off while I'm talking to you!" she demanded.

"Baby, you know I got to do what I got to do," he said as he stopped at the front door.

"I'm tired of hearing that muthafuckin' shit! That same lame-ass excuse!" KeeKee was yelling now.

PrettyBoy looked at her with a frown on his face, then he walked out of the house. KeeKee slammed the door as hard as she could behind him. Then she started to cry. She put her back against the wall and slid to the floor, crying her heart out, asking herself, "Why he won't change? Lord, please help him change, before it's too late."

Trai'Quan

Chapter 34
The show must go on!

Fulton Industrial Boulevard was a two lane up and down strip. The name said it all - industrial. There was all types of businesses outlining the street: hotels, fast food restaurants, and gas stations as well as warehouses where men worked hard labor for a little of nothing. The strip was also known for prostitution and drugs being moved inside and outside the hotels. The place was a hot spot for out-of-town truck drivers. To many of them, the strip was perfect. Maybe it was because of the strip clubs that were in the cuts off the strip, or maybe it was just being able to get drugs, rest, and a shot of pussy simultaneously.

PrettyBoy was familiar with the area, so he noticed the two hookers standing in the back of the Summit Hotel parking lot as he pulled up in his Benz CL500. The music was playing low in the car while he smoked a fat blunt of purple haze. 50 Cent's song "I'm Supposed to Die Tonight" played low in the car. He looked around in the parking lot to see if his partner BooBoo was there yet.

"Damn where the hell this nigga at!" He said out loud to himself as he backed the car into a vacant parking space. He sat back in his seat and watched the two women at work.

One was a white girl with long blond hair. She wore a burgundy top that had a V-neck showing off her DD breast, a short-ass patent leather skirt and some 6in heels. With her stood a black woman. She was about 6"2' in height. She was wearing heels, zebra stripe spandex pants, a black top, and a big fluffy wig. This one was an Amazon and she looked even bigger standing next to the small 5'4" white girl. They were having a conversation until they saw the Benz pull into the lot.

"Damn, bitch, you see that Benz?" Juicy, the black Amazon, asked.

"Shit, I wonder who up in that bitch," shot back Snow Bunny, the white blond.

"Girl, I bet that's a trick in there!" Juicy said with hope in her eyes. Then the woman stood there patiently waiting to catch their next customer.

Just then a white dude in a navy-blue Honda pulled up to where the two ladies were standing. PrettyBoy watched as the Amazon walked up to the Honda. He puffed on his blunt and blew out smoke.

"Where the fuck this nigga at?" he mumbled under his breath as he looked around. When he looked back towards the women, he said the Amazon getting into the passenger seat of the car, then the car pulled off. The white girl went to walking around advertising the goods.

PrettyBoy was too busy watching the hoes to even notice the figure that was creeping behind the car next to him. PrettyBoy opened the car door, got out, and made his way to the trunk. Just as he was lifting the trunk, he heard something move.

"Don't muthafuckin' move, nigga!" a voice instructed as Pretty-Boy stood still, completely flabbergasted.

"Now this can be just a robbery, or we can add murder to the muthafucka!" "Back away from the trunk!" he demanded.

PrettyBoy did just what he was told, and when he did, he got a good look at the robber. The robber wore a black ski mask. The masked man moved to the trunk of the car, reached in, and came out with a black book bag. He put the book bag on, never taking his eyes off PrettyBoy.

"Turn around, nigga!" he said to PrettyBoy.

He turned around like he was told. The whole time PrettyBoy was thinking, *Damn, this nigga seem young. I'm going to kill this little nigga!* Then he heard him run off.

The robber made a run for the building. PrettyBoy turned around and ran to the car for his Ruger 45 under the seat. He grabbed it just as the masked man ran past the white hooker. Snow Bunny saw him coming and saw what was going on and screamed. PrettyBoy zeroed in on him and he knew that he had a clean shot. He held the pistol and watched him get away. The robber turned past the building out of sight. PrettyBoy dropped the gun to his side. He shook his head while all types of things invaded his mind.

I really remember when I used to be where he at right now. I know I could have killed that young nigga, but what for? I ain't even gon' miss that li'l shit. I would have fronted the nigga that shit and told him come shop with me. I'm gon' let that nigga eat off me today. Man, I must be getting soft. Then again, somebody could have got my plates and that would have been a murder case. Now that would have cost a nigga. Man, fuck it.

He got inside his car. He set the pistol on his lap and left the door open with one of his legs hanging out. A white Ford Excursion, with black tinted windows, 26-inch chrome and white rims came around the corner into the parking lot. PrettyBoy got out of the car, leaving the door open with the gun in his hand swinging by his side. The Excursion pulled up next to him and the driver'' side window came down.

"What's the bizness, baby? What's up with the pistol?" BooBoo asked, not really knowing what was going on. BooBoo was dark-skinned and slim. He wore a white T-shirt and a red and black Atlanta Falcons football cap.

"Shit, my nigga, I was just cooling," PrettyBoy said, putting the gun in his waist. "Nigga, your slow ass took long enough."

BooBoo laughed. "You see why, don't you?" he asked, looking down towards his lap.

"What?" PrettyBoy said, walking up to the truck, then he peeked inside. When he looked inside, he saw the back of a woman's head giving BooBoo what seemed like the head of a lifetime.

"Ha! Oh yeah, I see why now, nigga," PrettyBoy said, laughing.

"So what's up?" BooBoo asked, ready to handle the business at hand.

"Man, you gon' have to give me the bread and I'll have Mike drop that shit off at your spot in a little bit," PrettyBoy said. "That's cool, right?"

"Yeah, nigga, but I thought you said you was going to have that shit with you," BooBoo said. He pulled the broad's head up from his lap by her hair. "Baby, hop in the back and grab that bag for me," he said to the girl.

"Shawty, I was, but something came up," PrettyBoy lied. Then he walked up and got the brown paper bag filled with stacks of money.

"Alright, my nigga," BooBoo said while handing him the bag.

"Mike gon' hit you up," PrettyBoy assured.

"Fuck with your boy," BooBoo said, backing the truck up. "I'll holla."

"Holla," PrettyBoy said as he pulled off.

Then he went to the car, got in, and pulled off, thinking to himself, *The show must go on!*

Chapter 35
Just dat fast

It was dark outside and later in the night when PrettyBoy decided to go home. He pulled his gray Mercedes Benz up into the driveway of his house in Buckhead. He sat in the car and stared at the house as he killed the engine.

Damn, he thought, *what went wrong?* The house was beautiful. With the big white columns, it reminded him of a mini version of the White House. But right now, he sho' didn't feel like the muthafuckin' president, and KeeKee wasn't acting like no First Lady. He had done everything for her. Now she wanted to start trippin'. He tried to rest his mind. He fired up a blunt while he sat outside in the car and thought.

KeeKee been acting real strange lately, kind of like she need some dick. That's what that bitch needs. I'll fuck the shit out of her two or three times a day from now on. Shit, have I not been handling my bizness? he thought as he pulled on the blunt. "Nall, I handles mine," he said to himself as a smile came to his face.

He saw the bedroom lights come on. He could see KeeKee's shadow as she walked through the room. "Why am I sitting out here? That's my baby and I love her, with her crazy, sexy ass." He put his blunt out in the ashtray. But just as he sat up straight, about to exit the vehicle…

Boom, boom, boom, boom, boom, boom.!

Bullets came ripping through the car's window, hitting him in the side and in the chest. PrettyBoy fell over in the passenger seat, shaking and coughing up blood.

A shadowy figure ran off into the darkness. Seconds later, the house door opened and KeeKee came running out. She ran to the car.

"Oooohhh my God!" she screamed. "Oh God, no!" She saw PrettyBoy's body jumping up and down while blood leaked from everywhere. She slung the door open and leaned over him. "Oh PrettyBoy, please don't die, baby, I'm sorry, I'm sorry, baby. I'm so sorry!" she cried as she saw his cell phone on the floor board and snatched it up to dial 911. "Hello, I need an ambulance. My boyfriend been shot!" she yelled into the phone as macabre thoughts invaded her mind, forcing her to mumble, "Not my baby! Lord, God, please don't take my man."

***

At the hospital, KeeKee sat in the hallway of the intensive care unit with her face in her hands. PrettyBoy had been rushed into surgery. The doctor said that he wasn't sure that he would make it because he'd lost a lot of blood. She couldn't believe what had happened. After seeing PrettyBoy like that, she deduced that she still loved him. She was so devastated that she didn't even hear Monica walking up.

"Girl, is he going to make it?" Monica asked with tears running down her face as she walked up.

KeeKee looked up, surprised, but happy to see her. "I don't know," she answered, crying the whole time. Then she stood up and they did their best to console one another. Both of the women hugged. "He in surgery now," KeeKee told her.

KeeKee was a sight to see, sitting in the hallway with her big white T-shirt on, covered in PrettyBoy's blood. One of the nurses had given her a blanket and it was draped around her now,

"Sit down, girl. I called Mike. He should be here in a minute," Monica informed as they both sat down. "What happened?" she asked KeeKee as she wiped her eyes.

"I don't know," KeeKee replied as she broke down and sobbed like a newborn baby.

"It's alright. It's gon' be alright. He gon' be alright," Monica said over and over again as she held KeeKee in her arms.

When Mike came onto the hospital floor, he saw them down the hall. He wore a dark brown Pelle Pelle leather jacket with a white T-shirt, dark brown Pelle Pelle pants, brown Timberland boots, a black and brown fitty cap, and a platinum chain, watch, and bracelet all filled with yellow diamonds. "What's up?" he asked, looking worried.

"They got brah in surgery, Mike!" Monica said while KeeKee continued to cry, not even acknowledging his presence.

"Damn, man," Mike said, pacing the floor. "KeeKee, what went down?" he asked, tryna see what the business was, but not wanting to disturb her any more than she already was.

"She don't know," Monica mumbled, answering for her.

"I'm sayin', where he was when he got hit up?" Mike questioned, trying to get some answers.

"Right outside the house. I was upstairs, then I heard some shots. I ran down and he was in the car all shot up," KeeKee managed to blurt out through tears.

"You ain't seen nobody? No car pull off or nothing?" asked Mike, in disbelief.

"Nall, I ain't' see nobody," she admitted, feeling extremely guilty.

"Damn. Ain't nobody know where y'all lived, unless they followed him home," he informed as KeeKee began to cry harder, her face now puffy and swollen from this encumber.

Monica held her in her arms. "Not right now, Mike!" she interrupted because she knew that KeeKee couldn't think straight at a time like this.

Minutes later, a doctor came out wearing a long white coat. He ambled towards them. "Ms. Johnson?" he stated, looking at KeeKee.

"Yes," she answered, looking up at the doctor with fear in her eyes.

Everyone became exceedingly quiet. You could hear a pin drop, a rat piss on cotton, or an ant dig a hole, as they all became attentive to the words of the doctor.

"We've taken three bullets from his chest. We were able to save his lung, and the other two went straight through. He's out of surgery and stable now. It looks as if he's going to be alright and he's going to make it," the doctor informed them, accommodating them all with a statement that was clear and to the point.

"Oh, thank you God, praise the name of the almighty!" screamed KeeKee as she and Monica hugged and shed tears of joy and elation.

"I told you, girl. PrettyBoy a strong nigga, he a fighter, alright" Monica said with joy.

"Thank you, Doctor," Mike said to the man as he shook his hand. "Can we see him?"

"Not right now. He's very weak and needs abundant rest. Tomorrow," finished the doctor, then walked away, leaving the Mac-11 crew to themselves as they cried tears of joy, and extolled the lord, praising him for sparing PrettyBoy's life.

Chapter 36
It's a dirty game!

Mike sat in a blue 2000 Grand Am rental car, parked right outside of PrettyBoy's house. He had positioned the car farther down the street so he could watch the house without being spotted by anybody coming or going from the place. He couldn't sleep last night after PrettyBoy got shot. He was distraught. That was his main man, his best friend. He had already lost Jarvis and Mac. He wasn't about to just sit back and do nothing. He decided he had to play detective, a street detective, and maybe, just maybe he could get some answers.

To him, KeeKee's story just didn't seem right. He felt like there was something up. In the streets, he learned at an early age not to trust anyone, that everybody is a suspect. He felt like the right way to commence his investigation was by going off of what he had, and what he had was KeeKee. So there he was at 9:30 a.m., sitting in a rental car, smoking a blunt filled with the best weed money could buy, watching for any signs of anything strange and peculiar happening. He wore the same clothes from the day before. The radio was playing the Tom Jorner morning talk show. He sat there playing with his cell phone for a while, then he placed it back into the case on his side.

Just then, KeeKee was coming out of the house. He looked up and noticed her. She had on a blue jean skirt, a royal, sky blue, and white Chanel top with sleeves that set the skirt off, and a pair of Prada heels to match her outfit. Her hair was still in two ponytails with sky and royal blue ties all the way down. She walked over to her sky-blue Benz truck and got in. Mike watched as she quickly backed out of the driveway. Once she pulled off down the street, he crunk up the rental car and followed her.

KeeKee was in the car listening to Trina's new CD as she rapped along. Well, just a little bit because she wasn't any good at rapping, plus it didn't help that she didn't know the words. She drove fast as she made her way through traffic. She rode for a while until she came to a side street and she turned on it, making a sharp right into a parking lot. The sign read Red Roof Inn. Mike parked across the street as he watched KeeKee park in front of a room door and get out of the truck.

He saw her knock on the door. Someone answered, and she went inside. He couldn't see the person who let her in the room.

"Damn, this dirty bitch!" Mike said out loud to himself. He was mad enough to annihilate a whole army as he stared at the hotel room in disbelief. He couldn't believe what he had just seen. What the fuck was KeeKee up to?

"Damn, after all the shit we done been through for this hoe, now she want to do my folks like this." Damn, life was full of surprises and this was definitely one. He would have never conjectured this shit, not even in a trillion years, and that's exactly what he deliberated on as he sat in the car. Just the thought of this disloyal bitch made him hit the steering wheel out of frustration. "Gotdamn punk-ass bitch!" he screamed. He looked at his iced out wrist watch. 9:45 a.m. He then looked back at the hotel. *She got to come back out*, he thought while staring at the room. He didn't care if he had to wait all day. It was going down.

***

The digital clock in the hotel room read 11:13 p.m.

KeeKee's legs were up in the air as she lay on her back butt ass naked. "Ummmm! Stttoooppp," she moaned with euphoria and pure pleasure as she pushed the head that was between her legs.

Tay looked up, licked his lips, and smiled as he looked into her beautiful and passionate eyes. She was covered in sweat. "You still mad at me, baby?" Tay asked her.

She smiled. "Boy, I couldn't be mad right now even if I wanted to," she joked with her body still pulsating from her back-to-back orgasms.

Tay crawled all the way onto the bed, positioning himself on top of her. He was also in his birthday suit. "Baby them five blocks I got from old boy was cool, but baby, that wasn't no money," he informed as he paused to kiss her neck. "We need to go ahead and get that safe that's in the house."

"Tay, you know I can't do that," KeeKee quickly shot back

"Yes, you can, baby," he reassured, kissing on her neck again. "It's me and you against the muthafuckin' world, baby." He planted more kisses around her neck, then worked his way down to her breasts while his hand slid down to her wet vagina.

"Baby, I...I...don't want to...do...that," she moaned as he palmed one of her beautiful breasts in his hand and went to sucking on her nipple. She moaned uncontrollably as she grew wetter and wetter by the second.

"Yes, you do, baby," Tay amended while licking around her nipple. Then he slid his hard rod inside her.

"Uhhhhh!" She creamed again upon his entry.

"Let's get this money," he insisted as he sped up his strokes, going deeper inside her.

"Ooohh, shit!" KeeKee said as Tay pumped away, ramming in and out of her, coercing her mind to comply with his every word and demand. "Okay! Ahhh, okay, I'll do it!"

***

3:27 p.m. was what Mike read when he looked at his watch. Mike was leaning back in the car's driver seat, trying to be patient, but he was tired as fuck. He had already smoked four blunts and now he could hear his stomach growling. He was hungry as a muthafucka. He was thinking about going across the street to the McDonalds that he could see from where he was parked, but just then, finally KeeKee came out, walking her li'l happy ass out of the hotel room skinning and grinning like a kid at the candy store. He saw Tay come out behind her. He had his shirt off with a platinum chain hanging from his neck, and he had a few tattoos. Mike could tell that the nigga was young. Mike watched as the two hugged and kissed in the doorway. Then she made her way to the truck and pulled off as Tay went back into the room and closed the door.

Mike watched as the Benz truck left the parking lot. Then he crunk up the rental car and drove over to the hotel. He parked a couple of spaces down from the room that he saw them in. He then reached up under the car seat and came out with a chrome colt 45. He looked around and didn't see anyone, so he got out of the car. He still had the gun in his hand as he walked up to the hotel room door. "Fuck this!" he said out loud to himself as he stood at the door. He kicked the door with all that he had.

The door almost came open, but Tay had put the security latch on. Mike kicked it again, sending it flying open.

***

Tay was sitting on the bed watching TV when he heard the door getting kicked in. He jumped up with surprised his eyes, but he quickly regrouped and ran for the gun that was laying on the table. As soon as he grabbed it, the door was kicked in, and Mike came clean on in just as Tay was about to turn around. Mike's gun was already raised, so he got the shot off first.

"Ahhhh!" Tay yelled immediately as he was shot in the ass and fell to the floor, dropping his gun. Mike walked straight up to him and put the pistol to his head, at the same time grabbing him by the neck.

"Ooohh man, don't kill me!" Tay begged pathetically.

"How the fuck do you know that bitch KeeKee, and when did you meet her nigga. How long?" Mike questioned him with words that shot out so fast, they overlapped each other,

"Man, what? I just met the bitch," Tay lied.

Boom!

"Ahhhh!" Tay screamed as he was shot in the leg. "Ooohhh shit, man!" he yelled as tears ran down his face from the excruciating pain.

"Muthafucka, if you lie again, you dead," Mike portended, madder than a muthafucka.

"She told me to rob her ole man to teach him a lesson. Something about the nigga ain't been showing her no love no mo'. Then the bitch got mad because the nigga didn't try to buck the robbery and she felt like to him, it wasn't nothing, so she had me shoot the nigga. Man, I didn't have no problem with nobody. She paid me. Man, it was the bitch!" Tay confessed through tears.

Mike heard a noise behind him and turned to look. The hotel room door was wide open, and a maid in a hotel maid uniform was peeking

144

in the room. Mike let off a couple of shots at the wall by the door. The lady screamed and ran away. Mike continued to stand over Tay as he pled for his tedious life.

"No, man!" Tay yelled as Mike pointed the gun at him

The last two words Tay heard in this world were, "Fuck you!" Three shots left his thoughts all over the floor.

Then Mike ran out of the room, jumped in the car, and sped off, thinking to himself, *One down, one to go…*

Trai'Quan

Chapter 37
If only you knew!

KeeKee had decided to go straight to see PrettyBoy. A lot was on her mind. She had some decisions to make. She looked worried as she made her way throw the sliding doors of the hospital, which always made her nervous as a stripper in church. That always gave her the creeps. The floors were shining and exceedingly spotless, but it was the funny smell.

KeeKee walked into the hospital room where PrettyBoy was. The room was dark and quiet, except for the noises that the machines made that they had him hooked up to. He was lying in the bed asleep when she walked into the room. He had an IV in his arm and some tubes coming out of his nose. She walked over to the curtains and pulled them back, letting some light shine inside the room. She just stared out of the window for a minute, tryin' to get her thoughts together. A tear rolled down her cheek.

PrettyBoy felt her presence in the room and opened his eyes, spotting her standing over by the window. "What's up, baby?" he asked in a very weak voice.

She turned around away from the window, wiping her tears.

"Baby, don't cry, I'm going to be alright. Come here," he said while lifting his hand, signaling for her to come to him.

She walked over to him, still crying, and laid on the bed next to him. He wiped her tears and kissed her softly on the cheek.

"I'm going to be alright, baby," he repeated, hating to see his girl so confusedfor his current dilemma.

"PrettyBoy!" she called his name just above a whisper.

"Yeah, baby?" he answered, as he ran his hand gently through her hair

"I'm sorry," she said, feeling remorse for her unknown and furtive actions.

"It's okay. Everything gon' be alright. It ain't your fault," he told her trying to help her relinquish the past.

"Yes, it is, baby, it's all my fault," she said, feeling guilty as she began to cry even harder. "I'm sorry, I'm so sorry, baby, I love you." She was on the verge of divulging the truth of the matter.

He looked into her eyes, trying desperately to appease her. He said, "Look, we gon' be alright, baby. I love you with all of my heart, and I don't want to live without you."

KeeKee hugged him, replying, "I love you too, baby"

They laid in each other's arms with the truth of the matter on the tip of KeeKee's tongue. She really wanted to tell him about everything, but she just couldn't find the right words, so she said nothing - nothing at all...

***

Mike pulled up in the hospital parking lot and parked the car. The parking lot was packed. He sat in the car for a while, tryin' to thinking everything through. "Man, what the fuck." He killed the engine and slowly got out of the car. He walked past a few cars, and that's when he happen to look over and he spotted KeeKee's truck parked over a couple of spaces in the parking lot.

Triflin'-ass bitch. The bitch might try to do something to PrettyBoy. He hastened his pace. He was walking with velocity now. He bumped into some man on the way in the hospital, almost knocking the man down.

"Hey," the man said, but Mike didn't pay him any attention. He was in a zone.

He walked to the elevator and pressed the button. He tapped his feet while waiting for it watching the numbers came down to the lobby. The doors came open. The elevator was empty. He got in the elevator and once the doors were closed, he pulled out his chrome Colt 45 and cocked it back. He make sure that he had one in the chamber that had KeeKee's name on it. Then he put the gun back on his waist, under his shirt, just before the elevator reached its peak.

The doors came open and he hurried out of the elevator. As he walked down the hall, murder was on his mind. When he got to Pretty-Boy's room, he slowed down. He walked through the door slowly. As he entered the room, he saw KeeKee, lying next to PrettyBoy in bed. They seemed asleep - both of them. The room was dim. A little bit of sunlight was shining in through the window. Mike walked over to a chair in the corner and sat down. He sat across from the bed. He just sat there and stared at them for a while. All he could think of was Kee-Kee's betrayal. She was playing both sides of the field, with the duplicity of Satan himself.

KeeKee finally looked up, spotting Mike in the corner. "Mike, I didn't even hear you come in," she said, a little surprised.

"Yeah," he said with a half frown, half smile.

She started to move in the bed, as she felt uncomfortable. "He's asleep," she whispered. "He's been doing a lot better, the doctor said."

Mike just looked at her, reticent.

KeeKee started to get up from the bed, and he stood up.

"Well, um, I'm going to give you some alone time with him." She stood there nervously while he just looked at her with abhorrence written all over his face. She walked over to the door and Mike followed her with his eyes. "Just tell him when he wakes up that I said I'll be back later tonight," she said before walking out.

When she made it out the room, she damn near took off running. She could feel it in her bones that something was wrong. "He knows. Mike knows!"

***

Mike slowly walked over to the bed where PrettyBoy laid. He looked down at his childhood friend, placing his hand on the rail of the bed. He hated to see his friend like this, and you could see the anger in his eyes. He looked at the machine, which told his heart beat.

"Yeah, playboy, you still alive," he said as he let a tear fall down his face. "Somebody should have told these bitch-ass niggas that a real nigga hard to kill," Mike confirmed as PrettyBoy opened his eyes.

"What up, nigga?" he said in a hoarse voice.

"What's up, boy?" Mike shot back, elated to have a dialogue with his right-hand man.

"Shit," PrettyBoy said, throwing a weak laugh. "Tryna shake those haters off!"

Mike laughed too. "You gon' be alright, nigga."

"Fo' sho'." PrettyBoy nodded his head.

"Man, check this out!" Mike said. "I been doing some homework. I found out who shot you, and I took care of it."

PrettyBoy shook his head again, knowing that if the shoe was on the other foot, he would've done the same thang.

"It's more. Man, look," Mike continued as PrettyBoy looked into his eyes, anticipating what his homie had compiled.

"What's up?" PrettyBoy said in a low voice.

"Man, I...um," Mike stuttered. "I know where them NY niggas hang at. It's only one muthafucka we need to get at, my nigga. That big muthafucka that got away when we hit that first lick. I feel like he had a lot to do with what happened with Jarvis," Mike offered, truly unwilling to break his friend's heart with the real dilemma at hand.

"Alright, my nigga," PrettyBoy said. "We gon' handle dat asap!"

"Well look, I'm gon' let you get some rest. I'm gon' fuck with you, shawty," he said as they gave each other pound. "One luv."

"One."

Mike walked towards the door, but before he could go out Pretty-Boy asked, "Where KeeKee at?"

Mike looked at his friend with sad eyes as he put a fake smile on his face. "Oh, she said she'll be back later tonight. She just left when I came in."

"Bet," PrettyBoy said, giving his friend a weak smile.

"Man, go to sleep," Mike instructed before walking out of the room. He knew how much his partner cared about KeeKee. He just didn't know that she didn't give a damn about him. The bitch couldn't have loved PrettyBoy. Shit, she tried to have his boy killed. He just couldn't take seeing his best friend heartbroken, not now, not while he lay in a hospital bed filled with bullet holes, and all because of this bitch, KeeKee. Damn, if that was love, Mike was glad that he didn't get involved with it. He thought of all the shit they had been through to save the bitch's life. They had lost Jarvis and Mac, and now PrettyBoy was almost killed. That no good bitch. She played the cross, then the double cross. Bitches could be worse than niggas sometimes.

Mike thought about all of this while he made his way down the hospital hallway, silently putting together a machination that would put an end to this whole facade, once and for all.

Trai'Quan

Chapter 38
It's a done deal

When KeeKee made it to the house she and PrettyBoy shared, she began to pack immediately. She was upstairs and had thrown most of her clothes out of the closet and onto the bed. She had so much stuff that she knew she couldn't take it all. She went to stuffing things into her Gucci bags and suitcases. "I got to get the fuck out of here," she said out loud to herself.

She was definitely in a rush. She packed two suitcases full of clothes and began to take them downstairs. They were heavy as fuck, so she just dragged them bitches down. She ran back up to the room and was about to go to the bathroom, when she stopped and thought about something else.

"Oh hell yeah," she said to the air as she made a move towards the dresser with the big mirror on it. She opened one of the bottom drawers, reaching under a few pairs of socks, and came out with a .380 pistol. She then jumped up, leaving the drawer open, and went to the closet. *Might need this shit*, KeeKee thought on her way to the closet. While in the closet she looked through her collection of fur coats that Pretty-Boy had bought her. She spotted her favorite one. It was pink and made like a jacket. She grabbed it. "You coming with me," she said putting, the coat on and walking out of the room with the pistol in her hand.

She slipped her hand inside the coat pocket on the way down the stairs. She felt something inside and pulled it out. It was a key. She stopped in her tracks. A light bulb went off in her head. It was the key to the safe that PrettyBoy kept in the closet. It was mounted inside the wall. KeeKee couldn't believe that she hadn't thought about it. She was too caught up in tryin' to make a fast escape. She turned and walked back into the room. She set the pistol down on the bed and made her way to the closet. She pushed and slid PrettyBoy's clothes along the racks until she found what she was looking for. The safe stared her back in the face. KeeKee used the key then pulled back on a lever and the safe came open. Neat stacks of hundred dollar bills lay perfectly in the safe.

"Ooohh shit!" KeeKee screamed out loud. She could tell that there was a couple hundred thousand there, maybe even a half a ticket.

She looked around the room for something to put the money in. She found an empty Gucci duffle bag on a top shelf. She grabbed it and started to stuff the money inside. The bag was half full and there was still money inside the safe. She couldn't get it all. She felt that it was time to go. It was a struggle picking the bag up and taking it down the stairs, but all that money was definitely motivation, and that's exactly what KeeKee needed as she threw the bag from around her shoulder to the floor, with the rest of her luggage. It was a shame she had to leave her beautiful dream house, she thought as she waved the loose hair from her face. She let out a breath of air as she headed to the kitchen to get a glass of water.

The ring of the doorbell stopped her. "Who the fuck could this be?" She walked over to the door, opening it without even looking out. "Mike!" KeeKee murmured, unable to conceal the fact that she was terrified.

"Ah, we need to talk," Mike said, pushing past her and walking into the house without even waiting for an answer. She backed out of the way as he placed his hand on the door and walked inside.

Damn, KeeKee thought as she closed the door.

The first thing he noticed were the bags. "Damn, you going on a trip or something?" Mike asked.

KeeKee's heart was racing. "Ah...um...I got to go see my grandma. PrettyBoy already knows," she managed to get out vapidly.

"Oh yeah? You must be staying for a while."

"Yeah, I'm going to stay for a little while. What you wanted to talk about, Mike? Because I was just about to catch my flight," she said as he stared at her.

Mike took his time answering, feeling a hard-on as he knew she was spooked to death. "Look, why don't we have a seat at the kitchen table," he insisted, thinking, *That way, your blood will be easier to clean up, bitch.*

Then he made a move towards the kitchen. KeeKee thought about the gun. *Damn.* She remembered leaving it on the bed upstairs. "Well, hold on, let me grab something from upstairs," she said moving towards the steps.

Mike peeped game and stopped in his tracks, then he turned around and made a step in her direction. "Hold up!" he said real fast, catching her in mid step. KeeKee froze before she even got to the stairs. "We can sit right here on the sofa and talk," he said, pointing his hand towards the sofa.

"Hold on, I'm just gon' run upstairs right quick," she said, really more like a plea. She could sense that something was about to go down and she was definitely not tryin' to catch the raw end.

"Nall!" Mike said with a serious look in his eyes. He was tired of playing games. He was ready to break this bitch off. "Let's stop muthafuckin' playing games, bitch!" he yelled belligerently.

KeeKee knew that it was now or never. She made a break for the stairs. But Mike was too fast for her. By the time she made it halfway up the stairs, he had grabbed her by the ankle, tripping her up and causing her to fall down hard.

"Come here, bitch. Where the fuck you think you going!" Mike yelled while he pulled her down the stairs.

She tried to fight to get away but that only ended up with her head hitting the steps, one by one, as she got dragged down them.

When Mike got her back into the living room, he grabbed her by her neck and brought her up to her feet. Then he slammed her into the wall and went to choking the shit out of her. He reached into his waist and pulled out the chrome Colt 45, the same gun he used to kill Tay's bitch ass with. He put the gun to KeeKee's head, still choking her with his other hand.

"Bitch, you ain't shit, punk-ass hoe!" he yelled, spitting in her face as he assailed his victim at hand.

KeeKee couldn't even breathe. She was tryin' to gasp for air, but fortunately, Mike loosened up his grip from around her neck just a little.

"Why, bitch? Huh? Why?" Mike yelled with no compunction for what he was doing to his best friend's other half.

"Mike, please, I'm sorry. Please...please don't kill me," KeeKee begged as she saw death around the corner.

"Sorry? Sorry, bitch? Sorry to me!" he yelled. "PrettyBoy the one you had shot, bitch." He pressed the gun harder to her head, ready to blow a hole in her temple.

KeeKee was terrified. She didn't want her life to end like this. The sad part was that she didn't even know why she had done it herself. At first, it seemed that she wanted to teach PrettyBoy a lesson by making him lose money, but then she got carried away. She knew she loved PrettyBoy and after seeing him in the condition he was in, and she hated herself for what she had done. She had tried to tell him, more than once, but deep down inside, she knew that the truth would never be able to come out. Hell, who would want a woman who tried to have you killed? KeeKee knew that PrettyBoy would probably kill her himself, if he ever found out. She knew her time was running out, so she had to think fast.

"It was you who I wanted to be with!" she said to Mike, desperately trying yet another innovation in hopes of saving her life.

It caught Mike off guard. He just stared at her for a minute. "What, bitch?" he said, perplexed.

"You heard me. Just being around you makes my pussy get wet," KeeKee said seductively.

He leaned his head to her ear and said, "Who the fuck you think you tryin' to play?"

KeeKee stared into his eyes, refusing to give in or up on her machination. "I ain't playing. Fuck that nigga. We can have all this shit. I just want you to fuck me right. See Mike, with you, I can be myself, and that's all I want, baby," she said, using her sexiest voice.

Then she leaned closer to him. Slowly she kissed him. Mike tried to resist at first, but then slowly he started to kissing her back. Slowly, his mind went from kill mode to drill mode as he let the gun drop to his side. KeeKee played with her tongue, pushing it in and out of his mouth.

Then she pulled away and said, "Let me treat you right, baby." She dropped to her knees, thinking to herself, *I know if I put this fire-ass head on Mike, he'll love me for the rest of his life.*

She began to undo his belt, and just when she got his fly open, she felt something cold and hard up against her head. As she looked up into Mike's eyes, she couldn't believe what she saw: death.

Boom!

Trai'Quan

Chapter 39
Blind shot

The next morning, the sun had just begun to rise, and the birds were beginning to chirp. A man wearing a Nike windbreaker and black jeans with a hat pulled down tight on his face walked into Piedmont hospital. He walked through the double doors and made his way to the elevator. Once he got on and made it to the floor he was seeking, he got off. He ambled down the hallway and walked up to PrettyBoy's room. The door was closed. He put his hand on the door and was about to walk in.

"Excuse me, sir," said a nurse standing in the hallway.

He looked at her, taking his hand away from the door.

"He can't have visitors yet. You have to come back later."

"Oh, okay," he replied as he walked off.

The nurse thought to herself that he looked quite peculiar for some reason as she watched him walk down the hall. Then she turned around and walked into the break room, where they kept the coffee.

The man saw her walk off , so he turned around and walked back towards the room, and this time, he walked straight in. The room was dim and the only sound he heard was the noises from the machines. PrettyBoy was asleep. The man took a couple of steps closer to the bed. Then he reached in his jacket pocket and came out with a 38 snub nose revolver.

Boom, boom, boom, boom!

He filled PrettyBoy with shots. The man ran from the room.

"Ahhhhh!" the nurse screamed as she ran into the room. "Oh my God. Somebody get a doctor!" she yelled out of the door, then she stood there, holding her hands to her mouth, flabbergasted as she witnessed PrettyBoy's guts, head, and body parts blown all over the room, with so much blood in sight that you would've thought it was a Freddy Kreuger movie.

***

Monica was just walking into the lobby of the hospital. She had decided to stop by early and pay PrettyBoy a visit. She had brought him breakfast – McDonalds, his favorite - because she knows how much he probably hated eating that hospital food. Plus she felt that it would be nice for them to have some time to talk alone. She wanted to pour her heart out to him and try to convince him to get out of the game. Too many people had died or been hurt, and she felt that it would continue to go on if someone didn't stop it. She loved him like a brother, and she didn't want to lose him too. So today, they were going to have a heart-to-heart talk, and Monica was hoping that he would see things her way, even if it took her coming down here every morning talking to him, because that's exactly what she was concocted to do . That was the only thing that was on Monica's mind as she made her way through the hospital lobby. Once she reached the elevator, the door was just opening and a dude came out fast. He ran right into Monica and almost knocked her down.

"Gotdamn, nigga. Watch where the fuck you going!" Monica yelled to his back, because the man kept going like he didn't give a fuck. "Bitch!" Monica mumbled as she got on the elevator and pressed the button. She was glad she didn't drop PrettyBoy's breakfast. Some people were just demented, she thought as she finally reached her floor.

As she got off the elevator, she noticed a lot of commotion going on down the hall. People were running back and forth, and doctors and nurses were everywhere. Then, as she got closer, she noticed that all the commotion was coming from PrettyBoy's room.

"Oh my God!" Monica yelled as she dropped the food from her hands, running to the room. When she got there, she saw a doctor standing over PrettyBoy yelling "clear", then pumping up and down on his chest. Blood was everywhere. The machine was flat-lining.

Monica threw her hands to her face as tears rolled down her cheeks. Then she finally let out a scream "Oh my God! No, no, no!"

One of the doctors yelled, "Get her out of here!"

Then a nurse grabbed her just as she was about to break down and sit on the floor.

"Come on, Miss, you don't need to be in here now. You can wait out here. I'm sorry, please," the nurse said as she pulled Monica through the doorway. She got into the hallway and cried like a newborn baby.

"What happened? What happened?" Monica cried out.

The nurse tried to comfort her while she informed her on what happened. "He was shot again. Someone came into the hospital and shot him. I'm sorry."

"No, why, God, why!" Hearing what had happened made Monica be turmoil. She then pulled away from the lady. "No, no!" she yelled with a broken heart as she took off running down the hall, not knowing where she was going or what she would do now.

Trai'Quan

Chapter 40
The final chapter

Monica sat on the passenger side of Mike's BMW crying as she looked out of the window, just staring off into space. Mike sat in the driver's seat with tears in his eyes. He wore a gray Balmains top and bottom set with a pair of gray Timberland boots. He was iced out like always, plus he had on a pair of Cartier frames with a Bossman skull cap broke sideways on his head. Monica wore a white and green Chanel dress that was very short. She wore blue jeans underneath the dress with a pair of heels to match. She also wore a pretty little diamond necklace.

"Man, I can't believe this shit!" Mike said, finally breaking the silence. They were sitting outside Monica's apartment complex, Century 21, in Cobb County on Six Flags Drive. The buildings were white with a little trace of blue.

Monica said, through tears, "I saw him on the bed filled with holes. PrettyBoy dead, Mike. He dead!" She cried uncontrollably.

Mike leaned his head up against the window and shed a couple of tears of his own, but he quickly wiped them away. He sat up and put his hand on Monica's. "It's gon' be alright, baby girl," he assured as Monica looked at him and gripped his hand. "Look, we got to hang in there. We got to be strong. If not for ourselves, then for PrettyBoy."

This made Monica do what she knew she had to do. She wiped her eyes and tried to be strong. "You're right," she agreed, "we gotta keep our heads."

Mike looked into her eyes. "I heard they be in the Bluff and fucks with that heroin. Baby girl, what you want to do?" Mike asked with malice in his eyes.

"Mike, you already know. Let's go kill these pussy niggas!" Monica, said infuriated and ready to get vengeance.

"Check this out. Go in the house and get right, then meet me on MLK at the Right Stuff gas station in about 45 minutes. We gon' go handle this shit for PrettyBoy," he said with murder on his agenda.

"For PrettyBoy!" Monica agreed as she got out of the car.

Mike crunk up the BMW and pulled off as Monica made her way to the building, thinking to herself, *Since these muthafuckas want smoke, I'ma set a fire.*

***

Monica, was at the Right Stuff gas station, sitting in her white 2003 Volvo on 20-inch rims. She was ready for war. She wore an army green suit with some black Timberland Boots. She had her hair pulled back into a ponytail. Two chrome 38 snub nose revolvers were in each of her pockets and she had an AR-15 laying on the back seat of the Volvo, plus she had filled one of her cargo pockets with bullets. She was ready and her adrenaline was pumping as she waited for Mike. She was look-ing at every car that pulled into the parking lot.

A '73 Impala pulled into the lot. The car was old and in desperate need of a paint job. It was a dirty green and it didn't have any hubcaps. One look at it and you would think that the car was a piece of junk. The car was a hoopty, but it had an excellent motor. Monica would have never guessed that it was Mike, until he pulled up beside her and signal for her to get in the car. Monica got out of her car quickly grabbing the AR off the back seat and jumped in with Mike.

"Look, baby girl, I found out that the niggas trap out of one of these houses. It's going to be plenty of niggas around, so if we just ride up and start shooting and shit, it could get ugly," Mike informed while Monica listened. "So I got a plan. We gon' post up in they hood and knock these bitches off as soon as we peep how they movin', you feel me? We gon' see the best way that we can hit these niggas and dip," Mike finished as the car made its way to the Bluff.

"That's what's up," Monica said, psyching herself out, tryin' to get in her zone.

Mike wore all-black army pants with Timb boots, a white T-shirt over a bulletproof vest, and a black baseball cap, no jewelry. He had two 40 Ruger handguns in his pockets so that they hung out, and a 223 was tucked away in the trunk.

When he and Monica made it to the Bluff, people were walking everywhere along the street. It looked like a block party, so they rode through until Mike pulled up by the house that he was looking for.

"That the one right there!" He pointed it out to Monica with his eyes as they slowly rode past.

There were two dudes standing on the front porch smoking, and they watched as the car passed. Mike rode around the block and turned on the next street. Then they sat in the car ducked off where they could see the house. Mike looked around. He noticed that there were a couple of people across the street standing in a little dirt area, a couple of nig-gas about his age. He watched as a junkie walked up to one of the guys and exchanged something. Shit, they were parked across from a trap. This was where the dope got sold.

"Look!" Monica said, getting his attention, pointing towards the house.

GridLock came out on the porch with a burgundy silk shirt on and a black derby hat with a cigar in his mouth. He also had on black slacks and burgundy alligator shoes.

"He must be the big man," Monica said more as a statement than anything else.

"That's the muthafucka right there!" Mike said, angry and sur-prised. He reached into the back seat and grabbed a bulletproof vest. He handed it to Monica. "Here, put this on."

Monica took off her shirt. She had on a dark green tank top with a brown sports bra underneath. She put the vest on and was about to put back on her shirt before Mike said. "Don't even bother putting that shit back on." Mike had just seen the dudes across the street leave except one. "Look, I want you to take the car up the street, past the house, then turn around and stop on your way back and light the muthafucka up. Hit whoever the fuck you can and make your way back right here to pick me up. But while you doing that, I'm going to get out right here and run up through the backyards and come out from the side of the house, letting them niggas have it at the same time. You just park down there at the other end of the street until you see me come out, and we move at the same time. Then I'll meet you back here after I make sure that nigga dead. You with me?" Mike finished, laying out the battle plan.

"I got you. Let's do this shit!" Monica shouted, hyped up and ready to take her body count to a whole other level.

"Let's do it," Mike said as he got out of the car and walked towards the spot where he saw the crack sale being made and Monica climbed over to the same side of the street as the house.

There was one dude out there, and he had just sold another rock to a lady junkie. Mike walked up as she walked off. He was about to walk past the nigga.

"Aye, playboy, it's enough money around here for everybody, but this me here, partner," old boy said, tryna flex his muscle on Mike.

Mike walked up to him, "Say what my nigga?"

"Nigga, you mutha——"

He never had a chance to finish before Mike had one of the 40s pushed up against his stomach.

"Man you got it," the man said, seeing the murder that was in Mike's eyes.

Mike could tell that he was a young nigga plus a pussy, because he was about to cry. He rubbed around his waist to make sure he wasn't strapped. Then he pushed the kid, "Get the fuck on!" Mike ordered just after he slapped the nigga across the head with the 40 one good time.

The boy took off running, holding his head as blood gushed out of his now split forehead. Mike jogged threw some trees into a nearby backyard.

Monica was up the street in the car. She was waiting to see Mike come beside the house. She wouldn't take her eyes off the house, she sat there and watched as Gridlock and the others stood on the porch. The more she watched GridLock smiling and talking, the madder she was getting. Finally, she felt that she couldn't wait any longer.

"Man fuck this!" Monica said, driving down the street towards the house. Her heart was beating fast, but she felt like fuck it, it's an eye for an eye a tooth for a tooth, and she was going to have her revenge. When the car came in front of the house, the guys looked as Monica brought the car to a screeching stop. She jumped out with the two chrome revolvers up, letting them sing, round after round.

She hit the two dudes, one in the chest and the other one she shot in the face. The .38 snub nose literally knocked off his whole nose. Monica yelled, "Die, muthafucka, die, muthafucka, die!" while she was shooting.

GridLock managed to drop to the floor and crawl into the house. After Monica saw GridLock make it inside of the house, she ran after him. It may have been the bulletproof vest that made her feel invincible, or maybe it was just the love for her lost friend, but regardless of the matter, right now, Monica wanted to kill this muthafucka, and nothing could stop her.

Once she got to the porch, she saw the two she had shot laid out. One was dead and the other one was on the ground spitting up blood, jerking up and down. He was still alive. Monica stood over him and fixed that problem. Boom! Then she put her back against the wall and peeked inside the house. She then dropped her used rounds to the floor and dug in her cargo pocket for more bullets. Just then, Mike ran up with his two guns in hand.

"What the fuck happened?" he asked as he walked up on the porch, being vigilant of the massacre before him.

"The big nigga in the house!" Monica said as she reloaded her guns, eager to chase after her target.

"Alright, wait in the car, I got this shit!" Mike snapped, tryna keep Monica out of harm's way and also get his guns just as dirty as hers.

Monica dashed into the house with her Dirty Harry's in hand, searching for her man. Mike went in behind her with his guns raised. The living room was empty. \

"You go upstairs. I'll check the kitchen and the basement!" Mike said, moving fast.

She didn't ask any questions. Mike went into the kitchen and nobody was in there, so he turned around and made his way throw the basement door.

Monica slowly made her way up the stairs with the guns leading the way. The steps made a sound. The next thing she knew, a man jumped out and shot at her from the top of the stairs. Close call, but he missed. She shot back. He fell down and didn't move. She tried to hurry up on the threshold, but before she did, another dude stepped out with a 12-gauge pump. "Bloom" he shot, hitting Monica right in the chest. The blast knocked her all the way down to the bottom of the stairs. She lay at the bottom. She wasn't dead, but she was unconscious - until the man walked down the stairs and blew her brains out.

***

Mike had just made it to the bottom of the stairs in the basement when he heard the shooting, and he quickly ran back up the stairs. He had to make sure that Monica was okay. The basement was dark and the place smelled like there was a dead rat (or body) in there. Mike couldn't see all the way through the room. That's probably why he almost didn't notice the movement down underneath the basement stairs.

"Aye!" the voice called to Mike.

He stopped and looked down and was about to shoot, but it was too late. GridLock stood under the stairs gripping the AK-47 he held pointed right at Mike. He let the chopper rip as Mike tried to make his escape.

The bullets ripped through Mike. He let off shots, going wild before he tumbled down the stairs. He still had one of his guns in his hand as he lay on the floor of the basement, shaking, and coughing up blood. He squeezed the trigger, letting off wild shots as he slowly drifted off into a place of darkness. Finally, the gun emptied. He died with his hand on the trigger.

GridLock walked out from behind the stairs and stood over his body, looking down at him in disdain. Then he spit on the body, and let him have it again.

Rat tat tat tat!

***

Three months later

After the deaths of the leaders of the clique, the name Mac-11, no longer rang in the stress. Others had picked up where they had left off. One thing was for sure, even when the players die out, the game itself lives on. For when there is death, there is also life. The drugs will forever be sold, there will always be attacks, and there will always be someone young or old, man or woman out looking for a quick way to get paid. The streets will always continue to create, as long as there is life to walk on them.

PrettyBoy's legacy was nothing more than a memory, like so many other hustlers that came before him. Now the stories, the names, and the people were nothing more than a legend, a conversation that people would bring up in the barbershop of the hood on the corner, or maybe kids who wanted to grow up and be big time drug dealers, fascinated by the lifestyle. But, no one really knew the price that was paid. Someone would be lying if they told you that the streets slowed down since PrettyBoy and his crew died, because the streets never slow down, they only speed up.

Tonight wasn't any different from any other Saturday night. The night life was very alive, and club SO was as packed as ever. Women stood outside in all shapes and sizes, waiting to get into the club. The ballers pulled up in their foreign and exquisite whips like always. It was the ATL, and ain't shit changed but the weather.

A sky-blue Chrysler 300 with chrome all over it, and 22in chrome rims, with black 5% tinted windows, pulled into the club's parking lot. The car came to a stop, and when it did, all the ladies stared. The door came open and went up in the air. The car had Lamborghini doors. Out of the car stepped a red fox. The ladies were all disappointed and turned their heads, discontented.

The red foxy lady walked away from the car after she let the door down. Boy, and was it a walk! She wore a black Dolce and Gabbana dress that clung to her body like a baby on a bottle. She had on the perfect heels to match and a pair of Gucci shades. When she walked, it was provocative. Her hips swung from side to side. It was enough to make a man dizzy. All the fellas' eyes were on her. She walked as if she was on a mission paying no one any attention. She walked straight up to the VIP line, paid, and tipped the bouncer.

"Damn, baby, you might need me to protect you tonight," one of the bouncers shot as he checked her out.

She gave him a weak smile, then she walked on into the club.

The club was jumping. The dance floor was crowded. The bartender was an older black man with a bald head and a beard. He stood behind the bar. She made her way over to the bar, sitting down on a stool and crossing her legs.

"What it is, hoe, what's up, can a playa…" The DJ played Trillville's new song.

"Love is in the air," she said to the bartender.

The bartender looked around to see if anybody was listening. Then he made her a quick drink and handed it to her. She took the drink and started to sip.

"Tell your boy I said I'll get in touch," the bartender informed, then looked over at the dance floor and said to her, "Your man upstairs." Then he smiled and moved down, wiping the bar as he went.

She set the drink down and walked through the crowded dance floor headed to the VIP area. There was a bouncer standing at the red rope, keeping people from walking through, but he opened the rope with no problem as he saw her walking up and she walked straight in and headed up the stairs.

When she got to the top, she noticed that the VIP room was also crowded. People were sitting on the sofas and chairs, drinking champagne having a good time. She walked past everyone and headed towards the back of the room. When she got to the round table, GridLock was being accommodated by three young ladies with a big cigar in his mouth. He was laughing while touching one of the girls. He didn't look up until she already had the .357 snub nose revolver out from the hip holster she was wearing, which now was pointed straight at his chest. He looked up, completely astounded, as he never anticipated this one.

"This for PrettyBoy. Mac-11 bitch!!" she yelled over the music before filling him with holes.

She emptied the chamber into his chest. He fell over and died, right then and there, as his blood splattered on all three of his female companions.

Everybody jumped up, running and screaming from the VIP section. She put the gun back in the holster, threw her hands up, and ran screaming with the crowd. She did this all the way out of the club doors until she reached the parking lot. As soon as she hit the parking lot, she straightened up and went back to her seductive walk, slow, sexy, and easy. She walked over to the car, slung the door up, got in, and pulled the door right back down.

"Ahhhh," she let out a breath of air, rejoicing out loud. "Easy as pie." Then a smile came to her face while she and PrettyBoy locked eyes in the rearview mirror, where he smiled from the back seat, screaming, "Mac-11 niggas never die. Our bodies may perish, but our souls, our souls will forever, roam the streets…"

"You going to see somethings that's going to make it hard to smile," Tupac said when his and Biggie Smalls song "Running" came on the car's system.

Red crunk up the car and pulled off, knowing that she was now officially The New Queen of Atlanta, and she was determined to have her way, shining brighter than the sun on a hot and humid summer day.

The END

Philippian: 3-10,11
"That I may know him, and the power of
his resurrection, and the fellowship of his suffering
being made comfortable unto his death,
if by any means I might attain unto the
resurrection of the dead."

-The Holy Bible-

Lock Down Publications and Ca$h Presents assisted publishing packages.

BASIC PACKAGE $499
Editing
Cover Design
Formatting

UPGRADED PACKAGE $800
Typing
Editing
Cover Design
Formatting

ADVANCE PACKAGE $1,200
Typing
Editing
Cover Design
Formatting
Copyright registration
Proofreading
Upload book to Amazon

LDP SUPREME PACKAGE $1,500
Typing
Editing
Cover Design
Formatting
Copyright registration
Proofreading
Set up Amazon account
Upload book to Amazon
Advertise on LDP Amazon and Facebook page

***Other services available upon request. Additional charges may apply
Lock Down Publications
P.O. Box 944
Stockbridge, GA 30281-9998
Phone # 470 303-9761

Submission Guideline

Submit the first three chapters of your completed manuscript to ldpsubmissions@gmail.com, subject line: Your book's title. The manuscript must be in a .doc file and sent as an attachment. Document should be in Times New Roman, double spaced and in size 12 font. Also, provide your synopsis and full contact information. If sending multiple submissions, they must each be in a separate email.

Have a story but no way to send it electronically? You can still submit to LDP/Ca$h Presents. Send in the first three chapters, written or typed, of your completed manuscript to:

LDP: Submissions Dept
Po Box 944
Stockbridge, Ga 30281

DO NOT send original manuscript. Must be a duplicate.

Provide your synopsis and a cover letter containing your full contact information.

Thanks for considering LDP and Ca$h Presents.

<u>NEW RELEASES</u>

SOUL OF A HUSTLER, HEART OF A KILLER by
SAYNOMORE
THE STREETS NEVER LET GO 3 by ROBERT BAPTISTE
RICH $AVAGE 2 by MARTELL "TROUBLESOME" BOLDEN
A GANGSTA'S PARADISE by TRAI'QUAN

STRAIGHT BEAST MODE III

De'Kari

KINGPIN KILLAZ IV

STREET KINGS III

PAID IN BLOOD III

CARTEL KILLAZ IV

DOPE GODS III

Hood Rich

SINS OF A HUSTLA II

ASAD

RICH $AVAGE III

By Martell Troublesome Bolden

YAYO V

Bred In The Game 2

S. Allen

THE STREETS WILL TALK II

By Yolanda Moore

SON OF A DOPE FIEND III

HEAVEN GOT A GHETTO II

SKI MASK MONEY II

By Renta

LOYALTY AIN'T PROMISED III

By Keith Williams

I'M NOTHING WITHOUT HIS LOVE II

SINS OF A THUG II

TO THE THUG I LOVED BEFORE II

IN A HUSTLER I TRUST II

By Monet Dragun

QUIET MONEY IV

EXTENDED CLIP III

A Gangsta's Paradise

THUG LIFE IV

By **Trai'Quan**

THE STREETS MADE ME IV

By **Larry D. Wright**

IF YOU CROSS ME ONCE II

ANGEL IV

By **Anthony Fields**

THE STREETS WILL NEVER CLOSE IV

By K'ajji

HARD AND RUTHLESS III

KILLA KOUNTY III

By Khufu

MONEY GAME III

By Smoove Dolla

JACK BOYS VS DOPE BOYS II

A GANGSTA'S QUR'AN V

COKE GIRLZ II

COKE BOYS II

By Romell Tukes

MURDA WAS THE CASE II

Elijah R. Freeman

THE STREETS NEVER LET GO III

By Robert Baptiste

AN UNFORESEEN LOVE IV

By **Meesha**

KING OF THE TRENCHES III
by **GHOST & TRANAY ADAMS**

MONEY MAFIA II

By **Jibril Williams**

QUEEN OF THE ZOO III

Trai'Quan

By **Black Migo**
VICIOUS LOYALTY III
By **Kingpen**
A GANGSTA'S PAIN III
By **J-Blunt**
CONFESSIONS OF A JACKBOY III
By **Nicholas Lock**
GRIMEY WAYS III
By **Ray Vinci**
KING KILLA II
By **Vincent "Vitto" Holloway**
BETRAYAL OF A THUG II
By **Fre$h**
THE MURDER QUEENS II
By **Michael Gallon**
THE BIRTH OF A GANGSTER III
By **Delmont Player**
TREAL LOVE II
By **Le'Monica Jackson**
FOR THE LOVE OF BLOOD II
By **Jamel Mitchell**
RAN OFF ON DA PLUG II
By **Paper Boi Rari**
HOOD CONSIGLIERE II
By **Keese**
PRETTY GIRLS DO NASTY THINGS II
By **Nicole Goosby**
PROTÉGÉ OF A LEGEND II
By **Corey Robinson**
IT'S JUST ME AND YOU II

A Gangsta's Paradise

By Ah'Million
BORN IN THE GRAVE II
By Self Made Tay

<u>Available Now</u>

RESTRAINING ORDER **I & II**
By **CA$H & Coffee**
LOVE KNOWS NO BOUNDARIES **I II & III**
By **Coffee**
RAISED AS A GOON I, II, III & IV
BRED BY THE SLUMS I, II, III
BLAST FOR ME I & II
ROTTEN TO THE CORE I II III
A BRONX TALE I, II, III
DUFFLE BAG CARTEL I II III IV V VI
HEARTLESS GOON I II III IV V
A SAVAGE DOPEBOY I II
DRUG LORDS I II III
CUTTHROAT MAFIA I II
KING OF THE TRENCHES
By **Ghost**
LAY IT DOWN **I & II**
LAST OF A DYING BREED I II
BLOOD STAINS OF A SHOTTA I & II III
By **Jamaica**
LOYAL TO THE GAME I II III

181

Trai'Quan

LIFE OF SIN I, II III
By **TJ & Jelissa**
BLOODY COMMAS I & II
SKI MASK CARTEL I II & III
KING OF NEW YORK I II,III IV V
RISE TO POWER I II III
COKE KINGS I II III IV V
BORN HEARTLESS I II III IV
KING OF THE TRAP I II
By **T.J. Edwards**
IF LOVING HIM IS WRONG…I & II
LOVE ME EVEN WHEN IT HURTS I II III
By **Jelissa**
WHEN THE STREETS CLAP BACK I & II III
THE HEART OF A SAVAGE I II III IV
MONEY MAFIA
LOYAL TO THE SOIL I II III
By **Jibril Williams**
A DISTINGUISHED THUG STOLE MY HEART I II & III
LOVE SHOULDN'T HURT I II III IV
RENEGADE BOYS I II III IV
PAID IN KARMA I II III
SAVAGE STORMS I II III
AN UNFORESEEN LOVE I II III
By **Meesha**
A GANGSTER'S CODE I &, II III
A GANGSTER'S SYN I II III
THE SAVAGE LIFE I II III
CHAINED TO THE STREETS I II III
BLOOD ON THE MONEY I II III

A Gangsta's Paradise

A GANGSTA'S PAIN I II

By J-Blunt

PUSH IT TO THE LIMIT

By **Bre' Hayes**

BLOOD OF A BOSS **I, II, III, IV, V**

SHADOWS OF THE GAME

TRAP BASTARD

By **Askari**

THE STREETS BLEED MURDER **I, II & III**

THE HEART OF A GANGSTA I II& III

By **Jerry Jackson**

CUM FOR ME I II III IV V VI VII VIII

An **LDP Erotica Collaboration**

BRIDE OF A HUSTLA **I II & II**

THE FETTI GIRLS **I, II& III**

CORRUPTED BY A GANGSTA I, II III, IV

BLINDED BY HIS LOVE

THE PRICE YOU PAY FOR LOVE I, II ,III

DOPE GIRL MAGIC I II III

By **Destiny Skai**

WHEN A GOOD GIRL GOES BAD

By **Adrienne**

THE COST OF LOYALTY I II III

By Kweli

A GANGSTER'S REVENGE **I II III & IV**

THE BOSS MAN'S DAUGHTERS I II III IV V

A SAVAGE LOVE **I & II**

BAE BELONGS TO ME I II

A HUSTLER'S DECEIT I, II, III

WHAT BAD BITCHES DO I, II, III

Trai'Quan

SOUL OF A MONSTER I II III
KILL ZONE
A DOPE BOY'S QUEEN I II III
TIL DEATH
By **Aryanna**
A KINGPIN'S AMBITON
A KINGPIN'S AMBITION **II**
I MURDER FOR THE DOUGH
By **Ambitious**
TRUE SAVAGE I II III IV V VI VII
DOPE BOY MAGIC I, II, III
MIDNIGHT CARTEL I II III
CITY OF KINGZ I II
NIGHTMARE ON SILENT AVE
THE PLUG OF LIL MEXICO II
CLASSIC CITY
By **Chris Green**
A DOPEBOY'S PRAYER
By **Eddie "Wolf" Lee**
THE KING CARTEL **I, II & III**
By **Frank Gresham**
THESE NIGGAS AIN'T LOYAL **I, II & III**
By **Nikki Tee**
GANGSTA SHYT **I II &III**
By **CATO**
THE ULTIMATE BETRAYAL
By **Phoenix**
BOSS'N UP **I , II & III**
By **Royal Nicole**
I LOVE YOU TO DEATH

A Gangsta's Paradise

By **Destiny J**
I RIDE FOR MY HITTA
I STILL RIDE FOR MY HITTA
By **Misty Holt**
LOVE & CHASIN' PAPER
By **Qay Crockett**
TO DIE IN VAIN
SINS OF A HUSTLA
By **ASAD**
BROOKLYN HUSTLAZ
By **Boogsy Morina**
BROOKLYN ON LOCK I & II
By **Sonovia**
GANGSTA CITY
By **Teddy Duke**
A DRUG KING AND HIS DIAMOND I & II III
A DOPEMAN'S RICHES
HER MAN, MINE'S TOO I, II
CASH MONEY HO'S
THE WIFEY I USED TO BE I II
PRETTY GIRLS DO NASTY THINGS
By Nicole Goosby
TRAPHOUSE KING **I II & III**
KINGPIN KILLAZ I II III
STREET KINGS I II
PAID IN BLOOD **I II**
CARTEL KILLAZ I II III
DOPE GODS I II
By **Hood Rich**
LIPSTICK KILLAH **I, II, III**

Trai'Quan

CRIME OF PASSION I II & III
FRIEND OR FOE I II III
By **Mimi**
STEADY MOBBN' **I, II, III**
THE STREETS STAINED MY SOUL I II III
By **Marcellus Allen**
WHO SHOT YA **I, II, III**
SON OF A DOPE FIEND I II
HEAVEN GOT A GHETTO
SKI MASK MONEY
Renta
GORILLAZ IN THE BAY **I II III IV**
TEARS OF A GANGSTA I II
3X KRAZY I II
STRAIGHT BEAST MODE I II
DE'KARI
TRIGGADALE I II III
MURDAROBER WAS THE CASE
Elijah R. Freeman
GOD BLESS THE TRAPPERS I, II, III
THESE SCANDALOUS STREETS I, II, III
FEAR MY GANGSTA I, II, III IV, V
THESE STREETS DON'T LOVE NOBODY I, II
BURY ME A G I, II, III, IV, V
A GANGSTA'S EMPIRE I, II, III, IV
THE DOPEMAN'S BODYGAURD I II
THE REALEST KILLAZ I II III
THE LAST OF THE OGS I II III
Tranay Adams
THE STREETS ARE CALLING

186

A Gangsta's Paradise

Duquie Wilson
MARRIED TO A BOSS I II III
By Destiny Skai & Chris Green
KINGZ OF THE GAME I II III IV V VI
Playa Ray
SLAUGHTER GANG I II III
RUTHLESS HEART I II III
By Willie Slaughter
FUK SHYT
By Blakk Diamond
DON'T F#CK WITH MY HEART I II
By Linnea
ADDICTED TO THE DRAMA I II III
IN THE ARM OF HIS BOSS II
By Jamila
YAYO I II III IV
A SHOOTER'S AMBITION I II
BRED IN THE GAME
By S. Allen
TRAP GOD I II III
RICH $AVAGE I II
MONEY IN THE GRAVE I II III
By Martell Troublesome Bolden
FOREVER GANGSTA
GLOCKS ON SATIN SHEETS I II
By Adrian Dulan
TOE TAGZ I II III IV
LEVELS TO THIS SHYT I II
IT'S JUST ME AND YOU
By Ah'Million

KINGPIN DREAMS I II III

RAN OFF ON DA PLUG

By Paper Boi Rari

CONFESSIONS OF A GANGSTA I II III IV

CONFESSIONS OF A JACKBOY I II

By Nicholas Lock

I'M NOTHING WITHOUT HIS LOVE

SINS OF A THUG

TO THE THUG I LOVED BEFORE

A GANGSTA SAVED XMAS

IN A HUSTLER I TRUST

By Monet Dragun

CAUGHT UP IN THE LIFE I II III

THE STREETS NEVER LET GO I II

By Robert Baptiste

NEW TO THE GAME I II III

MONEY, MURDER & MEMORIES I II III

By **Malik D. Rice**

LIFE OF A SAVAGE I II III

A GANGSTA'S QUR'AN I II III IV

MURDA SEASON I II III

GANGLAND CARTEL I II III

CHI'RAQ GANGSTAS I II III

KILLERS ON ELM STREET I II III

JACK BOYZ N DA BRONX I II III

A DOPEBOY'S DREAM I II III

JACK BOYS VS DOPE BOYS

COKE GIRLZ

COKE BOYS

By Romell Tukes

A Gangsta's Paradise

LOYALTY AIN'T PROMISED I II

By Keith Williams

QUIET MONEY I II III

THUG LIFE I II III

EXTENDED CLIP I II

A GANGSTA'S PARADISE

By **Trai'Quan**

THE STREETS MADE ME I II III

By **Larry D. Wright**

THE ULTIMATE SACRIFICE I, II, III, IV, V, VI

KHADIFI

IF YOU CROSS ME ONCE

ANGEL I II III

IN THE BLINK OF AN EYE

By **Anthony Fields**

THE LIFE OF A HOOD STAR

By Ca$h & Rashia Wilson

THE STREETS WILL NEVER CLOSE I II III

By K'ajji

CREAM I II III

THE STREETS WILL TALK

By Yolanda Moore

NIGHTMARES OF A HUSTLA I II III

By King Dream

CONCRETE KILLA I II III

VICIOUS LOYALTY I II

By Kingpen

HARD AND RUTHLESS I II

MOB TOWN 251

THE BILLIONAIRE BENTLEYS I II III

Trai'Quan

By Von Diesel
GHOST MOB
Stilloan Robinson
MOB TIES I II III IV V VI
SOUL OF A HUSTLER, HEART OF A KILLER
By SayNoMore
BODYMORE MURDERLAND I II III
THE BIRTH OF A GANGSTER I II
By Delmont Player
FOR THE LOVE OF A BOSS
By C. D. Blue
MOBBED UP I II III IV
THE BRICK MAN I II III IV
THE COCAINE PRINCESS I II III IV V
By King Rio
KILLA KOUNTY I II III
By Khufu
MONEY GAME I II
By Smoove Dolla
A GANGSTA'S KARMA I II
By FLAME
KING OF THE TRENCHES I II
by **GHOST & TRANAY ADAMS**
QUEEN OF THE ZOO I II
By **Black Migo**
GRIMEY WAYS I II
By Ray Vinci
XMAS WITH AN ATL SHOOTER
By Ca$h & Destiny Skai
KING KILLA

A Gangsta's Paradise

By Vincent "Vitto" Holloway
BETRAYAL OF A THUG
By Fre$h
THE MURDER QUEENS
By Michael Gallon
TREAL LOVE
By Le'Monica Jackson
FOR THE LOVE OF BLOOD
By Jamel Mitchell
HOOD CONSIGLIERE
By Keese
PROTÉGÉ OF A LEGEND
By Corey Robinson
BORN IN THE GRAVE
By Self Made Tay
MOAN IN MY MOUTH
By XTASY

BOOKS BY LDP'S CEO, CA$H

TRUST IN NO MAN

TRUST IN NO MAN 2

TRUST IN NO MAN 3

BONDED BY BLOOD

SHORTY GOT A THUG

THUGS CRY

THUGS CRY 2

THUGS CRY 3

TRUST NO BITCH

TRUST NO BITCH 2

TRUST NO BITCH 3

TIL MY CASKET DROPS

RESTRAINING ORDER

RESTRAINING ORDER 2

IN LOVE WITH A CONVICT

LIFE OF A HOOD STAR

XMAS WITH AN ATL SHOOTER

A Gangsta's Paradise